I turned on the light to my room and gasped. My parents had all the equipment out—the ion meters and recorders and even the thermal camera. They brought the thermal along only if they felt confident that it would capture something on-screen. Something paranormal.

Dad set the thermal reader down on my bed. "It's time we showed you something," he said.

I couldn't help feeling dread. Dad turned on a video screen. I immediately recognized the Courtyard Café in Charleston.

"Do you see those white shapes?" he asked.

I sucked in my breath. "What is it?"

Mom shook her head. "We're not sure yet. But Charlotte, whatever they are, it appears they followed us home."

"What do you mean? What are you talking about?"

Dad turned to me. "We think something powerful was triggered back in Charleston. We're getting readings stronger than anything we've ever recorded."

My legs felt shaky and I gripped the back of Dad's chair. The still images on the screen stared back at me. "Do you know what caused it?" I asked. No one said anything. I looked at Mom. "What triggered it?"

"You did," she said gently. "We think you're the trigger."

Also available from Mara Purnhagen and Harlequin TEEN

Tagged

And watch for more books in the Past Midnight series

One Hundred Candles
Available March 2011

Beyond the Grave
Available September 2011

past midnight

mara purnhagen

HARLEQUIN® TEEN

HARLEQUIN®
TEEN

ISBN-13: 978-0-373-21020-6

PAST MIDNIGHT

Copyright © 2010 by Mara Purnhagen

Recycling programs for this product may not exist in your area.

This edition published by arrangement with Harlequin Books S.A.

For questions and comments about the quality of this book please contact us at Customer_eCare@Harlequin.ca.

® and TM are trademarks of the publisher. Trademarks indicated with ® are registered in the United States Patent and Trademark Office, the Canadian Trade Marks Office and in other countries.

www.HarlequinTEEN.com

Printed in U.S.A.

ACKNOWLEDGMENTS

A sincere thank-you to my wonderful agent, Tina Wexler,
and equally wonderful editor, Tara Parsons.

A round of applause to
Ed Davis, Marguerite Demarse, Karen and Patrick Dulzer,
Heather Foy, Kimm Gildea, John and Martha Lohrstorfer,
Nancy McDaniel, Rita Owen and Kathy Payerchin.

A standing ovation to Robert Lettrick (Web site guru)
and Kristi Purnhagen, who read the first draft.

And a special shout-out to my guys:
Joe, Henry, Quinn and Elias, who keep me busy,
make me proud and remind me that I am never alone.

Dedicated to four people who have always lived far from normal:
Sayrah, Christine, John-Paul and Matthew

I know a lot about ghosts. More than the average person and way, way more than any other seventeen-year-old. Except for Jared and Avery, but most of what they know they learned from me this year, when things got crazy. I know a lot about things going crazy, too, thanks to my parents. They're paranormal researchers, and let's just say they like to bring their work home with them. And sometimes, their work follows them home.

For good.

one

I was never normal, but I liked to pretend that I was. It usually took a few months before everyone else caught on. School would start out just fine, then Halloween would roll around, my parents would be all over the local news, and suddenly I would find myself exposed as Charlotte Silver, Princess of the Paranormal. I don't know why I thought this year would be any different, but I did. And maybe it was different, but not in the way I had hoped. If anything, it was much, much worse.

We had spent the summer in Charleston, South Carolina. My parents were producing another one of their documentaries, this one called *Haunted Hospitality*. They spent their days researching old hotels and restaurants that claimed to have ghosts, while I relaxed at the beach and took walking tours of the city with my sister Annalise, who was a sophomore at the College of Charleston. She worked part-time at one of the supposedly haunted local restaurants during her summer break.

"The only spooky thing about the place is my boss," she

told me as we spread towels out on the sand. "He can get a little handsy, if you know what I mean."

I didn't, but I could guess. Annalise was strikingly beautiful with large hazel eyes and glossy black hair, just like our mom. Growing up, everyone talked about how she would become a model, but she was just over five feet tall, which is definitely a drawback in the modeling industry. Still, my parents had used her a few times for reenactments in their documentaries. Annalise would pull her hair into a bun, slip on a white Victorian dress and walk slowly in front of a green screen. When special effects were added later, she would appear as a transparent figure floating above the floor. She made a great ghost, which was ironic because in real life she was the one everyone seemed to notice while I was the one who slipped by, barely detected.

While Annalise resembled Mom, I took after Dad—tall and wiry, with dark hair that hung so straight it was infuriating. There wasn't even the hint of a curl. I kept it just long enough to tuck behind my ears and secretly resented it when Annalise complained that her glossy locks were simply "too bouncy."

During our third week in Charleston we decided to spend the morning at Waterfront Park. It was a warm Friday in June, the breezy air tinged with the sharp scent of seawater and the shrieks of gliding gulls. We walked along the pier searching for a place to sit and watch the boats. Tourists occupied all of the wide wooden bench swings that lined the dock, so we waited until a couple laden with cameras lumbered to their feet, then claimed the swing as our own. We sat back and rocked slowly, enjoying a clear view of the docked cruise ships and darting birds.

"This is nice," I said, pushing down on my feet to sway the swing.

"Summers are the best," Annalise murmured. She sounded drowsy. I felt tired, too, and worried that we might both fall asleep on the swing and wake up hours later, our arms bubbling red with sunburn.

"Maybe we should walk down to the beach."

"Can't. We have to meet Mom and Dad in less than an hour, and it'll take that long to walk to the beach and back."

I stopped swinging. "They didn't say anything to me about filming a scene today."

Annalise smiled. "They called me this morning. They need more chum."

"Chum" was what we called anyone who was brought in specifically to draw out paranormal energy. Some people claimed that a ghost would appear only if a certain kind of person was present, such as a curious child or a pretty girl. I didn't have to guess what kind of person my parents needed, and I felt a familiar twinge of jealousy. I was never asked to serve as ghost bait. Maybe I should have been grateful, but part of me wondered if it was because our parents didn't think I was good-looking enough to attract the interest of some dead, disembodied guy. It was insulting, really. Of course, no one in my family truly believed in ghosts, but still. Before I could get myself too wound up, Annalise spoke.

"They said they needed you, too."

"Really?" Maybe I had been wrong. Maybe my parents did see me as chum.

"Mom said the sound guy is sick. She needs your help."

Of course. Need a beautiful girl to lure reluctant spirits from hiding? Call Annalise. Need a plain and reliable worker to pick up the slack? Call Charlotte. Or don't even call—just tell Annalise to drag her along. After all, I couldn't possibly have anything else to do on a summer afternoon. I shook my head.

"I've got to stop thinking like that," I muttered.

"Huh?"

I sighed and rocked the swing harder. "Nothing."

We sat a little while longer before strolling through the old section of town, our flip-flops slapping against the sidewalks. The air smelled like jasmine and felt cooler than it had been at the pier. Guys stopped to gawk at Annalise while I pretended not to notice. It was actually easy because there was so much to look at: the historic mansions, the moss-draped trees, the horse-drawn carriages pulling noisy tourists through the streets. I looked for black bolts on the outside of houses, the telltale sign that the structure had been damaged in the earthquake of 1886 but had survived. There was something amazing about those homes, I thought, that they had been strong enough to survive devastation and were still standing today. "It's so beautiful here," I sighed.

Annalise adjusted her bikini top. "Yeah? I forget. I guess I'm used to it, though."

I didn't think I would ever get used to living in a town like this, and I'd lived in a lot of places. Any time my parents received funding for one of their documentaries we picked up and moved, sometimes for just a few weeks. The place we had lived the longest was England, when I was four and Annalise was eight. Our parents spent a year researching ancient castles. I don't remember much about the trip, but my parents liked to tell stories about how Annalise and I climbed up dark towers and napped in basement torture chambers. Not exactly a typical childhood. Of course, we didn't have typical parents.

Mom and Dad met just after college. They'd both studied psychology at Ivy League schools and were attending a national conference when they bumped into each other—literally, Mom claims—outside a lecture about parapsychology. Neither one believed in ghosts or hauntings or telepathy or anything else about the field, but they were interested in one aspect: disproving it. Within a year, they'd married and had set about debunking some of the world's most famous ghost stories, from wailing women in hotel hallways to confused Civil War soldiers roaming empty fields. They cowrote a book, *Ghost of a Chance,* explaining the scientific causes of most "hauntings." Their careers took off, and soon they were being recognized as the world's foremost ghost debunkers. Then, when my mother was three months pregnant with me, something happened.

They were filming one of their documentaries inside an abandoned insane asylum. Dad was repositioning a camera when he felt something brush past his leg. When he looked down, he didn't see anything, but later, when he checked the tape on his thermal camera, it showed a small figure, about three feet tall, sliding past him. When Dad checked the sound readings and matched them to the exact time he felt something against his leg, a clear voice could be heard saying, "Pardon me."

I guess everything changed after that. It was the one thing my parents couldn't explain. Dad became obsessed with EVPs, or Electronic Voice Phenomena. They're sounds that are too low for a person to hear but can be picked up by recording devices. He found natural causes for some of them, like local radio interference, and proved many to be hoaxes, but he could never fully explain what had happened to him at the asylum that day.

Dad once told me that the trick is not to prove something is real, but to prove that it is not real. My parents spent their lives trying to prove things were *not* real, and for the most part, they were successful. Very successful, judging by their book sales and TV deals. But I wondered sometimes if what they really wanted was to believe beyond a doubt, to have a clear and absolute answer to the question of what happens after a person dies. Personally, I didn't think I wanted to know because there was nothing you could do to change it, but I could understand how the question consumed people.

By the time Annalise and I found the restaurant our parents were investigating, I was starving and my forehead felt slick with sweat. All I wanted was some lunch and a blast of air-conditioning. When I opened the door to the Courtyard Café, I instantly knew I'd get neither.

Inside the restaurant it was dark and stuffy. A few ceiling fans churned the thick air slowly, creating only a hot breeze. All the tables had been pushed against one wall, with the chairs stacked at the other end. I knew most of the crew and guessed the rest of the crowd consisted of employees waiting for something to happen.

"Girls! Thank goodness you're here." Mom rushed toward us. She was wearing her work clothes: a pair of khaki pants and a black T-shirt. "We're way behind schedule," Mom said to Annalise. "The owner is getting frustrated and we've had absolutely no readings today." Mom lowered her voice and nodded in the direction of a dark-haired woman standing in the corner. She was wearing a long apron with "Mrs. Paul" stitched across the front. "She claims this place has a green lady." Mom smirked. "Right."

Mom didn't believe in apparitions of any kind. She said people thought they saw something, and their brains tried to connect it to the familiar, and that in twenty years of research she'd never once confirmed an actual, stereotypical ghost.

Annalise smiled. "I'm here for whatever you need."

"Me, too," I chimed in. "Could I just grab some lunch first?"

Mom glanced at me. "No time. We'll go out to dinner later, though, okay? Great. You know where the sound equipment is, hon."

I trudged away to locate the boom mic while Annalise pulled a black T-shirt over her bikini top and got ready to serve as the day's chum. Everyone on the team wore a black shirt because it made it easier for the cameras to pick up light around a person. I was wearing a white cover-up over my bathing suit, but it didn't matter too much—the sound person always stood behind everyone else.

Dad came into the room and clapped his hands together. "Attention, please!" he said. "We're going to be moving into the next room. We'll set up and start rolling."

He saw me across the room and waved. I tried to wave back, but I was holding the boom mic and accidentally knocked Shane, our main camera guy, on the head.

"Watch it," he snapped, but when he saw it was me, he smiled. "Oh, hey, kid. Filling in?"

"Unfortunately." I sighed.

Shane had been with us for so long we considered him to be family. He was thirty, stocky and a devoted fan of low-budget horror movies. He was trying to film his own slasher flick when he met my parents, who promised him a steady paycheck and strange adventures, so he stayed with us instead of running off to Hollywood. Shane was the only crew member who had been with us since the beginning. Most people stayed with us for a project or two, then settled down somewhere like normal people. Shane was like us—definitely *not* normal.

We all moved as one slow, sweaty herd into the adjoining

room. As in the front room, all the tables and chairs had been stacked against the walls and the drapes had been pulled shut to make it darker. It took a second for me to register, but the room was much cooler than the first one. In fact, it was downright cold. Within minutes I had goosebumps.

"Do you have a sweatshirt I could borrow?" I whispered to Annalise.

She gave me a funny look. "There's one in my beach bag." She went to the corner of the room and came back holding a pink sweater. "Try this. It's long on me, so it just might fit you."

I carefully set the heavy equipment down and pulled on the sweater. It was a little short but it fit, and I began to feel slightly warmer.

Dad asked everyone to quiet down and get ready. Then he had Annalise stand in the middle of the room. After checking all the cameras twice, he gave her the signal to start talking.

"Hello," she said. Her voice was confident and friendly, as if she was simply introducing herself at a crowded party. "My name is Annalise and I'm wondering if anyone is here with us today."

One camera focused on Annalise while one stayed on my parents and the rest of the team. They held up their heat-sensing monitors and EMF (Electro Magnetic Field) readers while I positioned the microphone above their heads.

"Okay, we're getting something," Mom said. "It's faint, but it definitely wasn't here last night."

I felt my nose begin to tickle and knew a sneeze was coming on. I tried to hold my breath.

"Keep talking," Dad instructed. "I think it's working."

Annalise kept up her conversational tone, asking simple questions and then waiting a moment as if she expected an answer. My sneeze was building, I could feel it. I tried not to, but just as Annalise asked again if anyone was present, it happened. I sneezed so loudly that half the team jumped, startled, and the sound echoed off the walls. Dad shot me a disapproving look while a few people tried not to giggle.

"Sorry," I said, loud enough for the entire room to hear. "My bad."

"Charlotte, please, if you could just—" Mom was cut off by sudden activity on all the readers. "Wait a minute. We're getting something."

I could see the lights of the equipment dancing wildly. It was rare to get so much activity so quickly. My parents were smiling and everyone seemed excited.

Everyone but Annalise.

"Um, guys? Something feels weird." She looked around the room and grimaced.

"What's wrong, sweetie?" Mom asked.

"I don't know, but something's not right."

"Just a few more minutes, okay?"

I was watching my parents so I knew where to position the mic, but I was also keeping an eye on Annalise. Her open, casual demeanor was gone, and her patient smile had been replaced with a slight trembling, as if she was cold and scared at the same time. I had never seen her frightened before. In fact, I'd never seen anyone in my family scared. We were all rational, logical people who knew that a simple scientific reason was waiting to be discovered behind nearly everything. Something was causing massive activity in the room, but my parents would figure out what it was once they had collected all their data. Annalise had done this enough times to know that. But she was obviously freaked out. She shook her head and looked down.

"Please? I want to leave."

Dad was gazing at his EMF reader. "One more minute, hon."

Annalise swallowed. "I can't. I can't stay here one more minute. I'm done."

Mom and Dad exchanged a glance. "Sure, of course. You can go. We've got enough," Dad said, but he furrowed his brow. I knew he wanted as much recording time as he could get.

Mom walked over to me. "Go with her," she whispered. "I can take the mic."

I followed Annalise into the main dining area. She sat on the floor and covered her face with her hands. I sat next to her.

"You okay?"

She shook her head. "It was so strange, Charlotte," she whispered. "I mean, I was fine, and then suddenly I felt so—so *sad.*"

I rubbed her shoulder. "How do you feel now?"

She sniffed and looked up. Her eyes were slightly red. "Better, actually." She looked at me. "The second I left that room I felt a little better. I have goosebumps, though."

I pulled off the pink sweater she'd let me borrow. "Here. I stretched it out for you."

She laughed. "Thanks." She looked past me, toward the other room. "Did you feel anything? I mean, besides that you were cold?"

"No. And the cold I felt, well, that was just the room."

Annalise frowned. "But the room was warm. Hot, actually."

I thought my sister was out of sorts and I didn't want to disagree with her about temperature. We both knew that feeling cold was often a sign of paranormal energy, but we also knew that sometimes it was just that—cold. People often read too much into it.

Within a few minutes the team finished up, and we all helped put the tables and chairs back the way they had been, thanked Mrs. Paul for her time and headed out for a late lunch. Annalise remained quiet for most of the afternoon, and I tried to reassure her that everything was fine.

"Just think," I said. "You'll never have to step foot inside that place again."

I didn't know it then, but I was dead wrong.

two

It's all about energy. That's what my parents say, at least. The theory that drives them, the single idea that makes their career possible, is that ghosts do not exist but energy does. The way Dad explained it to me when I was little is still the way I like to imagine it. I had been having a hard time sleeping in the house we were renting at the time because I could hear footsteps pacing outside my door. Dad came in and sat on my bed.

"Think of time as an ocean," he said, smoothing my hair. "And think of yourself as a small stone tossed into that ocean. What happens when you throw a stone into water?"

"It sinks?" I wanted Dad to stay as long as possible so I wouldn't have to listen to the footsteps alone.

"Well, yes. But it also creates tiny ripples on the surface, doesn't it?"

"Yes."

Dad's theory was that some people created greater ripples than others. Their energy, he said, echoed long after they'd died. At first, he believed that only strong or intense emotions lingered, which was why places where a death had occurred seemed haunted. But then Mom discovered something that changed his mind.

Mom met Edith, a woman who lived down the street. Edith claimed that an evil spirit was trying to force her out of her home. "It grabs my feet at night," she said. "It tries to pull me out of my bed."

Edith was nearly hysterical. She'd been living in the house for only a few months and she didn't want to move, but the paranormal activity occurred every week, and she couldn't take much more. My parents investigated and noticed some strange readings in the master bedroom. While Dad spent a week at the house, Mom contacted the former owners, who had lived there for over thirty years before retiring to Florida. They'd never had a problem with anything strange, they said. Their daughter, now in her forties, still lived in town, and Mom invited her to the house one day.

"I loved this place," the woman said. "My family was so happy here."

Mom didn't tell the woman what had been happening, only that she was researching the history of the house. When they walked into the master bedroom, the woman told Mom how she used to wake up her parents every Sunday morning by running into their room.

"I'd grab their feet," she said. "I'd try to pull them out of bed so they'd get up and make me pancakes."

The revelation changed the way my parents looked at their research. They'd been working under the assumption that only people who died left behind energy, usually after a single powerful event. Now they realized that perhaps simple repetition could also leave an imprint. It explained doors opening, or the sound of footsteps. Their new goal was to determine what triggered such energy. Why didn't Edith feel the pull at her feet every single night or only on Sundays? They never figured it out completely, but they did introduce Edith to the woman and explained the story and their theory. The solution was actually easy: Edith moved her bed, and the tugging stopped. My parents reasoned that the trigger was the position of the bed because Edith had placed it in exactly the same spot as the previous owners.

"The truth is that the paranormal is normal. It's just a normal we don't understand yet," Dad liked to say.

I thought about Edith's story as my parents continued to investigate Charleston. They would spend a week at a place, filming in both the daytime and at night to get the best possible results. They tried to coax Annalise into returning to the Courtyard Café, but she refused. Mom and Dad backed off, but I knew they were just waiting, hoping that she would change her mind before the end of the summer.

Annalise and I spent the next few weeks of our vacation going to the beach or taking walking tours of the historic downtown. She didn't talk about what had happened and I didn't ask. I hated to see her so quiet, though. She wasn't simply my sister—she was my friend. We'd spent our lives moving from place to place and, besides my parents and Shane, Annalise was the only truly constant person in my life. Despite the fact that I sometimes felt overshadowed by her beauty and the attention she received, I was closer to her than anyone. I had missed her terribly when she left for school, and I knew I would miss her even more after the summer ended and we moved to our next destination while she began her junior year of college.

"Where are you guys going after this?" she asked me one afternoon. We'd stopped at a little park to enjoy a picnic lunch.

I was sitting against the trunk of a huge tree, eating pasta salad out of a paper bowl. Annalise was sitting cross-legged in the grass and poking at a Cobb salad with her plastic fork.

"No idea. They'd better figure it out soon, though. I need to register for school."

"You'll be a senior," Annalise said softly. "Wow. That's kind of hard to imagine." She fastened a foil lid on her bowl and set it inside the beach bag we'd brought. "How many high schools have you been to?"

I did a quick calculation. "Five? No—six. I guess Florida doesn't really count, though, because I was only there for a few weeks."

Annalise shook her head. "You know, it's not fair. To you, I mean. You should be able to stay in one place for more than a single semester."

I sighed. "That would be nice."

I had learned how to leave a place behind without leaving a piece of myself along with it, but more important, I had taught myself how to be detached. I never joined teams or clubs, and I doubted my picture appeared in a single yearbook. I was, in a way, a ghost: no one could prove I had ever existed once I physically left a location.

"You should say something," Annalise said. "I mean, aren't you tired of Mom and Dad dictating your life?"

"Why didn't *you* ever say something? You've been to more schools than I have."

"Honestly? It never even occurred to me that I had a choice."

"But you think I do?" I wasn't sure what my sister thought I could accomplish. Did she want me to pick a fight with our parents? Did she want all of us to move permanently to Charleston?

"I think that if we approached them together, we could change things."

"Change what things?" I wasn't sure I wanted to join Annalise's revolution. Things were fine. Not perfect, but fine. I could live with that.

"It's time we had a voice," Annalise said. "Whatever Mom and Dad want, they get. If they want to move across the country, they do. If they want you to stand in the middle of a room and allow negative energy to hurt you…" She didn't finish her sentence.

"What really happened?" I finally asked. She was plucking grass from the ground.

"I don't know, Charlotte. I really don't. But I don't want to feel that way ever again."

"What way?"

"I just felt this *sadness*. This terrible, awful sadness, and it seemed to come from inside me and fill me up until I could hardly breathe."

I watched my sister for a while. She was staring at the grass, slowly running her fingers over it. I wanted to help her get over the experience, and there was only one way I knew how to do that.

"You have to go back," I said.

"I was afraid you were going to say that."

"If you don't face it—whatever *it* is—it'll bother you. And you can't escape it, exactly, because you *live* here now. What if your friends decide to go to the Courtyard Café for lunch one day? You can't avoid this. Not forever."

"I know," Annalise said softly.

"We can go in the daytime, with the entire crew and everything, so you won't be alone."

"That didn't help me before."

"I'll be with you, too. I'll stand right next to you and I won't leave no matter what."

"I know you won't, Charlotte. But you didn't feel what I did. You're not afraid because you don't think anything's really going to happen."

She had me there. Annalise was the sensitive one in the family, a sponge soaking up other people's emotions. I was more like a slab of concrete. I believed she'd felt something, but I didn't think it was anything more than random energy. If she went back, maybe she'd realize that and she could stop feeling so frightened.

We sat in silence for a few more minutes. I knew she was coming to a decision and that I shouldn't push her. I looked around at the park where we were sitting and realized that we were just a block from the Courtyard Café. Horse-drawn carriages clopped steadily down the road while happy tourists snapped pictures and peered into the windows of specialty shops. Everything in Charleston felt so old, as if it was stained with history. I rested my head against the tree and wondered how long it had stood there. More than a century, I guessed. Its trunk was huge, and its thick branches curled up toward the sky.

Finally, Annalise looked at me. "You really think I should do this?"

"I do."

She stood up. "Okay, then. Let's get it over with."

Our parents were thrilled that Annalise had reconsidered, but revisiting the café proved to be difficult. Mrs. Paul, the restaurant's owner, had seen a surge in customers after my parents appeared on the local news and proclaimed the Court-yard Café "one of the most haunted locations in the city." We had to schedule a time when business was likely to be slower so we could close off the side room and not affect the dinner rush.

Two weeks later, right after the Fourth of July, we returned. Our visit was supposed to be short—less than an hour, Mrs. Paul declared—and we couldn't move any of the furniture. Dad grumbled that they'd done a lot for the business and this wasn't the way to be thanked, but Annalise was relieved—no matter what, the whole thing would be over and done with soon.

"Ready?" I asked her. We were sitting at a small table in the main room as the crew set up their equipment.

Annalise nodded. "Yeah. I mean, you can't ever be ready when you don't know what's about to happen, but I'm as ready as I can be."

We were wearing black T-shirts and khaki pants like everyone else. I'd grabbed my sister's pink sweater as we were heading out, just in case she got cold, and tied it around my waist as we walked into the side room. Both cameras were focused on us as Annalise and I weaved around the tables and made our way to the center of the room. I took hold of my sister's hand and squeezed. She smiled at me then began to speak out loud.

"Hello. My name is Annalise and I'd like to know if anyone is here with us today? If there's someone here, could you give us a sign?"

The room began to feel cooler to me, and I almost let go of my sister's hand so I could put on the sweater, but she was holding on to me tightly and I didn't want to pull away from her.

"How are the readings?" Mom whispered to someone.

"Normal so far."

"Keep talking," Dad directed.

Annalise took a deep breath. "Hello? Do you remember me? I was here a few weeks ago. I felt—something. Was it you? Is someone here?"

Nothing happened. Twenty minutes passed, and all the readings remained the same. I could tell my sister was feeling calmer because she began to loosen her grip on my hand. Maybe she thought her first encounter had been a fluke, a surge of energy that had nothing to do with her presence.

"See?" I whispered. "This isn't so bad."

I felt an icy breeze against my cheek and wondered if the air-conditioning had kicked on. I let go of Annalise and quickly slipped her sweater over my head.

"Charlotte." Annalise's voice was strained. "It's happening again."

"We're getting something!" Dad announced.

I grabbed my sister's hand. "I'm right here," I said. "Not going anywhere." Annalise nodded, but her face was frozen with panic. I decided to do the talking for her.

"Whoever you are, we mean no harm," I said loudly. "What do you want?"

I paused. Mom was holding a digital recorder to catch EVPs, and she nodded at me. I asked a few more questions, but as I did I was aware of two things. First, my sister looked pale and her hand was shaking. Second, something felt weird to me, as if the air had gotten heavier or somehow thicker. I didn't see anything strange, but I felt absolutely certain something was standing in front of us. It seemed to move closer, and I could feel a breath of frozen air against my cheek. Annalise whimpered.

"That's it," I declared. "We're done."

I pulled my sister with me, guiding her around the tables and chairs and various crew members. I didn't stop until we were standing on the front porch of the restaurant, where the frozen feeling from inside instantly melted away in the muggy evening air.

Annalise slumped onto the porch steps and immediately began to cry. "Did you feel it, too?" she asked. "Did you feel how awful it was?"

"I felt something," I admitted. "But it wasn't horrible. It was just—unusual, I guess."

Our parents came outside, and I was surprised to see that they were both smiling. "Great job, girls," Dad said. "I can't wait to listen to the EVPs from this one."

"The ion meter was all over the place," Mom added. "Highest numbers we've had so far."

"How wonderful for you," Annalise said bitterly.

Dad looked confused. "Are you okay?"

Annalise stood up. "No, I am not okay," she said, her voice loud. "You dragged me into something terrible and you don't even care. Well, I'm through. I'm never doing this again! Ever!" She stormed off before my parents could respond.

"What on earth was that all about?" Mom asked me.

I didn't have an answer. I'd never seen my sister react so furiously to one of my parents' sessions. I didn't know what was happening, but I had the uneasy sense that whatever it was had just begun.

three

When I was eight, we lived in a house where you could hear the steady squeaking of a rocking chair nearly every night, even though we didn't own a rocking chair. When I was ten, we lived in a house where the TV changed channels on its own so often that it was useless to sit down to try and watch something. And when I was thirteen, we lived in a house where you could hear violin music drifting up like smoke from the empty basement. I lived in all these places, and none of them truly scared me, although it could feel creepy at times. I would get ready to take a shower and then pause, wondering if something was watching me undress.

Mom and Dad were drawn to these places. The older, the better, and they often rented a house without having ever stepped inside. And although they constantly reassured us that it was all just random energy and nothing that could really hurt us, my sister and I longed for a new house, something completely devoid of history or rumors or sudden, unexplained deaths.

That's why, when Dad pulled the moving van into the driveway of 1227 Copper Court that August, I had to restrain myself from yelling with joy. It was everything I'd always wanted in a house, right down to the beige aluminum siding.

"We're home." Mom sighed. She was less than thrilled and had spent the two-hour drive from Charleston reminiscing about all of the other places we'd lived and how none of them had been less than a hundred years old. I'd spent the drive trying to tune out her stories and take a nap. I must have slept for a little while because I remembered dreaming about a dark-haired girl reading a book. She was wearing a long, old-fashioned dress as she sat against a tree, and I had the distinct impression that it was the same tree where Annalise and I had eaten lunch a month before. It was just a brief vision, but the image of the girl slowly turning the pages of her book stayed in my head until we arrived at our new house.

Both Mom and Dad sat in the van staring at the place we'd call home for the next ten months. It was so new the front yard hadn't been seeded yet. We'd be the first people to live in it. That thought alone made me smile.

"Who's got the keys?" I asked from the backseat. I couldn't wait to look around and claim my bedroom.

I nearly skipped to the front door while my parents slowly followed. Dad tossed me the keys and I stepped inside. Sunlight poured in from the bare windows.

"Smells like new carpet," I said happily.

"Smells like *cheap* carpet," Dad grumbled behind me.

Mom looked around at the taupe walls and white trim and brown doors. "This place has absolutely no personality," she announced. "I bet the interior of every house on this street looks exactly the same."

"That would make sense," Dad said. "All of the exteriors look exactly the same."

I wasn't going to allow their sour mood to affect my jubilant one. I ran upstairs, peeking into each of the three bedrooms until I decided on a room overlooking the backyard. It was smaller than the master, but it had more windows and a decent closet. I sat on the pristine carpet, leaned back on my arms and closed my eyes. This would be my room for at least one full school year. I couldn't believe my luck—or Annalise's ultimatum.

After her second experience at the Courtyard Café, Annalise retreated to her campus apartment and refused to speak to our parents for a few days. They seemed upset by her reaction, but they were too busy examining video footage and planning their next investigation to really do anything about it. They weren't prepared when Annalise showed up at their hotel room demanding a family meeting.

"Family meetings" were rare for us. Usually it meant my parents were going to announce the next city we'd be living in. My dad tried to take control right away.

"I know we need to discuss certain things," he began, "but I'd like to set a few ground rules first."

Annalise stopped him. "I have only one ground rule. You need to listen to me without interrupting for five minutes. Then you can say whatever you want."

My sister had never been so assertive. She meant business, and my parents knew it. They nodded and Annalise took a deep breath. She told them that she had always participated in their projects enthusiastically, but she would no longer do so unless they agreed to a few new conditions.

"What kind of conditions?" Mom asked warily.

Annalise reminded her of the five-minute rule, and Mom pretended to zip her mouth shut and throw away the key.

"First, I'm taking a year off from helping with any of your research."

Out of the corner of my eye, I saw Dad stiffen. I had overheard enough conversations during the past few days to know that he wanted to focus completely on the findings from the Courtyard Café, which had produced readings beyond their expectations. Instead of compiling all of the Charleston locations into one television special, he planned to dedicate a full hour just to the restaurant—and Annalise. He wanted to go back, and he needed her to go with him.

"Second, I will return to that place only in my own time, when I feel that I'm ready." Annalise looked directly at Dad when she said this. He sighed.

"Third, I want the three of you to stay in one place this year. Same town, same house, same school for Charlotte."

I don't know who was more surprised by the third condition: me or my parents. Annalise and I hadn't discussed "changing things" since our conversation in Charleston, which I thought was merely my sister venting. I honestly didn't think she would take action.

Before anyone could respond to her request, Annalise held up her hand.

"I know that may sound strange. But I have my reasons, if you'll just hear me out."

She went on to explain that college had proved to her how important it was to have some stability in her life. She had loved traveling when we were kids, but part of her always wanted to stay in one place longer, to make friends and join teams and just generally be a part of something.

"You were part of something," Dad protested. "You were a part of our crew."

"Are you saying we've been terrible parents?" asked Mom, her brow furrowed with worry.

"I'm saying that I want Charlotte to have a chance at something a little more normal." She smiled at me. "And no, I don't think you're terrible parents."

Mom and Dad were obviously perplexed. Dad said he had always thought traveling was the best education you could get.

Mom turned to me. "Is this what you want, Charlotte? Are you unhappy?"

It was strange how quickly the conversation had turned. I fidgeted nervously.

"It would be really nice if we could stay somewhere for a year," I said. "I think I'd like that."

Over the next few days, my parents seemed to forget about their research as they tried to come up with a plan that would make us all happy. They found a small town about two hours north of Charleston with a good school system. They planned trips to nearby cities with locations they could easily drive to. All that was left was to buy a house. That's when I stepped in.

"I have one condition of my own," I told them. They were looking up homes for sale online, and every picture on the screen showed some kind of dark Victorian. They weren't thrilled when I told them I wanted to live in a new house, but in the end, they agreed.

"We're doing this for you," Dad said with a shrug. "Might as well go all the way."

Mom smiled. "We're doing this for all of us," she said,

touching Dad's hand. "We want everyone on our team to be happy."

That was how I ended up sitting on the clean, brand-new floor of my clean, brand-new bedroom at the beginning of August. I was enjoying the empty space and the sun on my face when Mom came upstairs.

"I see you've claimed a room," she said, sitting down next to me.

"Isn't it perfect?" I asked. "I've always wanted something like this."

"Well, I'm glad. This house may not have much personality, but it certainly has a lot of light."

"I could sunbathe right here," I joked.

Mom patted my knee. "Enjoy. Then come downstairs. We have a lot of unpacking to do."

I groaned. Unpacking was the worst part about moving, especially since my parents always insisted we do it ourselves. They didn't trust anyone with their expensive equipment. Instead of putting it off, I decided to get the hard labor over with and followed Mom downstairs. Outside, Dad was surveying the open back of the moving truck.

"Do we have more stuff than before, or does it just seem that way?" he asked.

"Just seems that way," I said. "Hand me a box."

Over the next few hours I made a thousand trips up and down the stairs. My legs were feeling sore and I was ready for a break. I was happy, though, that my room now held a bed and a dresser, as well as a dozen different cardboard boxes marked with my name. I noticed one of the boxes was smaller than the others and was labeled in my sister's handwriting. I knelt down next to it and peeled off the thin brown packing tape. On top of everything was a single sheet of notebook paper.

Dear Charlotte,

I hope you're having fun settling into the new house (ha ha—I know how much you love to unpack). I just wanted to let you know how great it was to spend the summer with you. I've enclosed some things I thought you might need this year. Have a great time at school, and see you soon!

Love, Annalise.

I folded the note in half and smiled. It had been difficult leaving Annalise behind in Charleston. I had given her a wordless hug before getting into the car, but I refused to look out the window as she waved us off. Even though this would be her second year away at college, I still had not gotten used to the emptiness that came with her absence from my daily life. And now, after having spent the summer with her, I knew it would take me a while to readjust.

I sifted through the box and found a new alarm clock, some notebooks, a pack of multicolored pens and, at the very bottom, Annalise's pink sweater. I lifted it out and held it for a moment.

"Charlotte! We need your help!" Mom called from downstairs.

"Coming!" I yelled back.

"Charlotte."

I spun around. It sounded like Mom had whispered my name from right behind me, but no one was there.

"I need something to eat," I mumbled. My stomach was obviously impairing my brain. I set Annalise's sweater on top of the nearest box.

"There's no residual energy in a new house," I said out loud.

I waited, as if I might get a response. Nothing. I turned and went downstairs.

"Oh, good." Mom motioned me over to the truck. "I don't need to remind you to be careful with this," she said as she gingerly placed a TV monitor in my arms.

"Living room?" I asked, drooping under the weight of the monitor.

"Next to the others," Mom confirmed.

We never really had a living room in any of our houses. My parents converted the largest room of each home into their office, which meant pushing long tables against the walls and filling every square inch with equipment and computers. The dining room held the sofa and TV, and we ate our meals in the kitchen.

After all of the equipment had been safely stored in the living room/office, I returned to the truck, determined to get everything cleared out before dinner. As I was pulling out a floor lamp from the back of the truck, I spotted a girl about my age standing across the street. My first thought was to wonder how she had managed to put a guinea pig on a leash, but when I looked more closely I saw that she was walking a very tiny dog. She waved, so I set the lamp down on the sidewalk and crossed the empty street to say hi.

"Moving in?" she asked. Her microscopic dog began to bark wildly. It was more of a high-pitched squeak, a sound like something a rabid mouse would make.

"Yeah. Hi, I'm Charlotte."

"I'm Avery. And this—" she motioned to her pet "—this is Dante. Shh, Dante."

"What kind of dog is he?"

"A very naughty one. Dante!" She smiled at me apologetically. "He's normally friendly. And quiet." She scooped him up and cradled him in her arms. He stopped barking, but his eyes remained on me. I'd never seen a dog so protective of its owner.

"So, where are you moving from?" Avery asked. Her light brown hair was pulled into a ponytail and she wore a blue T-shirt with "Vikings" across the front.

"We just came from Charleston," I said.

"Oh! I have friends who go to college down there."

"My sister goes to school there! I wonder if she knows any of them?"

Avery nodded. "Maybe. It's a small school." She looked around. "Just like this is a small town. In fact, nearly half of last year's senior class is going to Charleston." She frowned as if she'd remembered something, then changed the subject.

We chatted for a while. She pointed out her house at the bottom of the hill and we talked about school, where we would both be seniors.

"Do you play any sports?" she asked.

"No. You?"

Avery pointed to her T-shirt. "I'm a cheerleader. Go Vikings."

I smiled. "Is this a big sports town?"

"Kind of. Our football team's good. They went to State last year. Although this year…" Her voice trailed off and she looked down at Dante, who was keeping up a low growl as he stared at me.

"So where's the best place for pizza around here?" I asked, deciding to change the subject this time. "My parents said I could pick dinner tonight."

"That's easy. There's this little place downtown called Giuseppe's. Best pizza around, I swear."

"Do they deliver?" After a long day of unpacking, I was craving a hot slice of pizza with pepperoni and extra cheese.

"No, but I'll go with you to pick it up," Avery offered. "I have a car."

I was thrilled. Not only was Avery nice, but she lived right on my street and had her own car. If we became friends, we could drive to school together and I wouldn't be forced to ride the dreaded bus. My parents owned two vehicles: a silver BMW that I wasn't allowed to go near, and a large black van with the word "Doubt" painted across the side in tall silver letters. I couldn't imagine pulling up to school in the van, so it was either catch a ride with someone or endure the school bus.

We agreed to meet an hour later. Dante squirmed in Avery's arms as she walked home, growling and trying to get one final, fierce look at me.

"I don't like that dog," I muttered. As soon as I said it, I felt a sharp, cold breeze against my face. It lasted only half a second, but it was so intense I put a hand to my cheek. Then Dad hollered at me to get the lamp off the sidewalk and into the house.

"I met a girl from my new school," I told him after I'd plugged the lamp into an outlet in the dining room. He was pushing a sofa against the wall. "We're going to get pizza later."

Mom came into the room carrying a fake fern. "You've made a friend already? That's wonderful."

I shrugged. "She's not a friend yet. But we'll both be seniors, so that's something."

"Bring me back a sausage, bacon and pepperoni," Dad grunted.

"Three-pig pizza. Got it."

Mom rolled her eyes. "I'll take a vegetarian with extra mushrooms."

I could hardly wait until Avery arrived. I went upstairs and took off my sweaty T-shirt, then debated for a while on what to wear. The sun was setting and my room was feeling cooler, so I decided to put on Annalise's pink sweater. It wasn't on the box where I'd left it, though. Instead, it had been folded and placed on my bed. I was annoyed that Mom had come in my room, even if it was just to fold a sweater. It was as if she was silently scolding me to keep things neat.

The doorbell rang and I bounded down the stairs. Mom got to the door first. "Hello, I'm Karen Silver," she said, her voice sounding exactly as it did on her TV specials.

"Avery Macintosh. I live down the street."

"We'll be back in an hour," I told Mom as I brushed past her.

"Have fun. Drive safe!"

I was embarrassed, but Avery nodded seriously. "I'm a *very* safe driver, Mrs. Silver. You don't have to worry."

Avery's car was an adorable green Mini Cooper. "I love it!" I said. "Is it new?"

We got in. "It was a present for my sixteenth birthday, future graduation and next three Christmases combined." Avery checked her rearview mirror, then looked over at me. "And I meant what I said—I'm a safe driver, so buckle up." She said it with a smile, but I could tell she wasn't joking around.

"Absolutely," I said, clicking the belt into place.

The drive took longer than I thought it would. Avery seemed to take a lot of deserted back roads instead of the main street that led downtown, but I told myself that I just didn't know the town or its shortcuts yet. When we finally arrived at Giuseppe's, I was starving. We slid into a corner booth and ordered a large cheese and pepperoni, and I placed a carryout order for my parents.

I looked around. "This is a neat place." It was tiny, with stone walls and arches that made it feel as if we were sitting inside a warm, well-lit cave. I breathed in the scent of garlic and a slightly woodsy aroma.

"They have an actual brick oven," Avery said. "That's what makes it so good. I come here all the time with people from school."

"Are you ready for school?" I asked her.

"Not really. Schedules come out next week, and I'm hoping I made the yearbook staff."

"I'm just hoping all my credits will transfer and I won't get stuck taking gym."

Avery sipped her drink. "So why'd you guys move here?"

I gave my standard response. "My parents' jobs."

The answer seemed to suffice, and Avery didn't ask anything else about it. She talked about our school, Lincoln High, and which teachers to avoid. "Seriously, if you get Abrams for math, try to get your schedule changed. All he does is yell."

Our pizza arrived and I was happy to discover that it was absolutely the best I'd ever had. "And I've been to Italy," I told Avery, "so I know what I'm talking about."

Avery put down her drink. "Really? That's so exciting! When were you there?"

I immediately wished I hadn't said anything. I didn't want her to think I was bragging, and I certainly didn't want my parents' career to come up. "It was a few years ago. We went there on vacation."

"I've always wanted to travel abroad," Avery said. "My

boyfriend went to Rome with his family last Christmas. He said it was amazing."

"What's your boyfriend's name?"

"Adam. He was a senior last year."

"So he's away at college now?"

"He got into Michigan."

I picked up my pizza. "That's far. But you can see him when he comes home to visit at holidays and stuff, right?"

Avery hesitated. "His family moved out of state a couple of months ago."

Her voice sounded heavier, and I realized her relationship with Adam was a difficult subject for her. I tried to think of something to say, but she beat me to it.

"What about you? Did you leave someone behind when you moved?"

"I wish." Moving around so much had meant that my love life was constantly interrupted. Even when I did date a guy, it never lasted more than a few weeks, and I didn't bother to keep in touch after my family left a place. What was the point? Eventually, I'd have to hear about how he'd met someone else, and I hated the idea of being so easily replaced.

Avery and I chatted and ate. I was just starting to feel really comfortable with our conversation when her cell phone rang. She pulled the phone out of her purse and checked the number.

"Sorry, it's my mom," she said. "I have to answer it."

I polished off another slice as Avery took the call. She asked a lot of questions, like "what?" and "when?" and I got the impression that something bad had happened. She flipped her phone shut.

"I'm so sorry, but we have to go."

"Is something wrong?"

She bit her lower lip. "It's Dante. My mom said he's really sick. I need to take him to the emergency vet."

"I'm sorry," I said. "I hope he's going to be okay." I offered to go to the vet with her, but Avery said no. We boxed the rest of our pizza and picked up my parents' order. On the way home, Avery drove on the main road back to our neighborhood, which took less than half the time and made me wonder why we had gone the long way to begin with.

"I hope Dante will be okay," I said again before I got out of the car. "If there's anything I can do, let me know."

"Thanks, Charlotte. I'll see you later."

I delivered the pizzas to my parents, who were in the living room discussing footage with Shane.

"I'll start with EVPs this time," Shane said as he reached for the meat pizza. "I think we got something at the restaurant."

"I'd like to hear it." Dad wiped his mouth with a napkin. "I want to determine if there was a correlation between the ion readings and possible EVPs."

I didn't want to listen to their boring conversation, so I went upstairs to unpack boxes of clothes. My room was cold, and if I didn't locate my own stuff, I would be wearing Annalise's sweater until it fell apart. As I sat on the floor and refolded some shirts, I couldn't shake the feeling that it was strange Avery's dog had gotten sick just hours after I had announced that I didn't like him. It made me feel as if I was somehow responsible.

"I don't hate Dante," I said out loud. "I want him to get better and be absolutely fine."

I waited for a cold breeze or warm, reassuring feeling, but nothing happened. I took a deep breath. What was wrong with me? Did I really believe I had the power to make dogs sick? Was I mental? Normal people didn't think that way.

I sat on my bed listening to the muffled voices coming from downstairs. It was my goal to get through the entire school year as someone who passed for normal. Ordinary, even. Making friends with Avery was a good start, I thought. If I could keep my parents from appearing on local TV and made sure they kept their big "Doubt" van hidden in the garage as much as possible, I might be okay. On the outside, at least. And wasn't that what mattered? You could have all the crazy thoughts you wanted, as long as you smiled and kept them to yourself. People saw only what you allowed them to see, and I planned on showing them Charlotte Silver, a regular, everyday kind of girl.

I hoped that this time, I could pull it off.

four

Annalise called me the day before school began to check in and wish me luck.

"Have you unpacked everything yet?" she asked.

I looked around my room. Half the boxes were empty, but I hadn't taken them downstairs yet. "Almost."

She laughed. "I'll take that as a no."

I told her all about Avery but left out Dante, whose condition had improved almost overnight.

"The vet said it must have been something he ate," Avery explained the day after we'd had pizza. "He's still sick, but he's much better than he was last night." She frowned. "I don't know what he could have eaten, though. He's too little to jump up on the counter or get into the trash."

I felt relieved—and more than a little silly that I'd ever thought Dante's sudden illness had anything to do with me. Random breezes and cold spots were just that—random.

"How's Charleston?" I asked Annalise. "More important, how are you?"

"I'm really good, actually. Don't take this the wrong way, but ever since you guys left, I've felt a hundred times better, as if a weight has been lifted off my chest." She grew quiet. "That awful feeling I had? It just kind of faded."

"I'm glad," I said, trying to stifle a yawn.

"Am I boring you?" Annalise joked.

"No. I guess I haven't been sleeping very well lately."

"I'll let you go, then. Rest up, Charlotte. And have a great first day."

After we hung up, I yawned again and glanced at the clock. It was only seven, which was way too early to go to bed, even if I was tired. I hadn't been staying up late, and I usually slept in until nine or ten, but I was still exhausted. I had been dreaming a lot lately, something that was rare for me. I couldn't remember the dreams when I woke up—they seemed to slip away from me like sand sifting through my fingers—but more than once I saw the same dark-haired girl reading by an old tree. I awoke feeling as if I'd just visited Charleston, and the sense that I was now in the wrong place would linger for hours afterward.

Looking around my room, I decided it was time to clear out some of the mess. I scooped up piles of dirty clothes, dropped them into empty boxes and carried one box at a time downstairs, emptying the clothes into the laundry room and flattening the boxes before stacking them in the recycling bin. On my third trip, I stopped to see what my parents were doing. They were in the living room with Shane, and the three of them had earphones on, which meant they were listening to EVPs.

"I've got something," Dad said loudly. Mom and Shane removed their headphones.

"From the Courtyard Café?" Shane asked.

"It's near the end." Dad clicked on his computer. The screen showed a voice-analysis screen, which allowed the user to see voice patterns and static. I walked into the room, curious to hear what they'd found. Mom turned around and saw me.

"Hi, Charlotte." Her voice was a little too loud, like she wanted to make sure Dad and Shane knew I was there. They stopped what they were doing and turned around, as well.

"What'd you find?" I asked. "Can I listen to it?"

Mom and Dad exchanged a glance, and Dad cleared his throat. "Of course you can," he said. "Just not yet. Let's wait until we have everything compiled. Then you can hear it all at once."

It was not the response I had been expecting. Normally my parents were more than eager to share their findings with me and to get my input. EVPs were usually just a few words, and sometimes they were so soft you could barely make out what, if anything, was being said. Our parents often asked Annalise and me to listen to recordings and give them our first impression. Most of the time, it was just a garble of noise, and our parents would try to prove that another source, such as radio interference, was causing it. Once in a while, though, they recorded a clear word, such as "help" or "hello." When this happened, they tended to guard it carefully, eliminating any possible explanation of its cause before presenting it to someone outside of the team.

Which was what they were doing now, I realized. When had I been demoted from "vital member of the team" to suspicious outsider?

"Fine. Well, I'm going to bed early, I guess. School tomorrow."

"Good luck!" Shane said happily.

"I'll get you up early," Mom said. "We can have breakfast together."

"Sure. Okay, then. I'm going upstairs."

The three of them nodded, still smiling, obviously waiting for me to leave the room before they returned to their findings. I walked slowly, hoping they would get back to work so that I might overhear something. When I reached the doorway, I glanced over my shoulder. They were still watching me.

"Good night, honey," Mom said.

"Sleep tight," added Dad.

"Whatever," I mumbled, retreating up the stairs. I knew they were listening to make sure I went all the way up to my room, so I stomped my feet for their benefit and shut the door to my bedroom with a little more force than necessary.

I was annoyed with my parents but didn't have time to dwell on it. Almost immediately after slamming my door, the phone rang.

"Ready for tomorrow?" It was Avery.

"Everyone keeps asking me that," I said, plopping down on the floor. I was pleased that I'd cleared so much out of my room, especially the mini mountains of clothes. I now felt more organized. Or, at the very least, not like a complete slob.

"I'm picking you up at seven-thirty sharp," Avery reminded me, emphasizing the word *sharp*. "What are you wearing?"

We had made a trip to the mall a few days earlier to shop for back-to-school clothes, which was fun because Avery had a talent for finding stuff that looked great on me without being pushy about it.

"I was planning on wearing those dark pencil jeans and that blue tank top you picked out."

"Perfect. I'm wearing my green shirt with that white denim skirt. What do you think?"

I knew Avery was asking me only as a courtesy, but I appreciated the effort. "Sounds great," I said.

Avery and I had spent a lot of time together over the past week. Besides the mall, we'd been back to Giuseppe's once for lunch and had run a few errands for her mom. She even tried to help me organize my closet one afternoon.

"You could hang everything by color," she suggested as she surveyed the piles of clothes scattered across my room.

"Or I could just do what I always do," I said, pointing. "Clean goes there and dirty goes over there."

She laughed. "What's that pile, then?"

"Almost dirty but clean enough to wear once more."

"This is a lost cause, I think." She rubbed her arms. "It's cold up here."

"I think this room gets most of the air-conditioning," I said. "I can open a window, if you want."

"No, that's okay. I'm thirsty. Let's go downstairs."

Avery had been over twice, but I'd never given her the full tour of my house. Part of me was embarrassed by all the boxes stacked in the corners, but I was more concerned about the questions she'd ask once she saw the living room. Sure enough, after we'd grabbed sodas out of the fridge, she caught a glimpse of the computers and monitors and the hundreds of gray, tangled wires.

"Wow. What's all this?"

"Oh. My parents make, um, documentaries," I stammered. "They edit everything from home and then send it to their production company."

"You're kidding. What kind of documentaries?"

"Well, they just finished up filming one about, um, historic buildings in Charleston. Pretty boring stuff."

That was basically true, I told myself. I hoped Avery didn't notice how much I was hesitating. I was an awkward liar.

"Hey, maybe they can help us." We had gone into the dining room to watch TV. "The cheerleaders are planning an amazing Homecoming week this year. We want to make a video postcard for the alumni. Maybe your folks could help us edit it?"

"Yeah, maybe. I'll ask them later."

My parents had been off at a nearby historical society in an attempt to gather information about local landmarks. I had no idea when they were coming back, but I really didn't want Avery around asking them any questions. They'd have no problem revealing everything to her, and I wasn't ready for that. So far, she saw me as a normal, slightly messy girl who trusted her fashion sense and liked pepperoni pizza. It was too soon to ask her to accept me as some sort of teenaged Ghostbuster, as well.

I was able to get Avery to leave before my parents came home, but I knew it wasn't something I could keep up for too long. Eventually, she would run into them and the truth would come out. We'd been living in the house for three weeks, though, and so far, so good. Shane had been driving the "Doubt" van and kept it parked at his new apartment across town, and my parents were fully occupied with editing their Charleston footage.

Avery and I talked a little more about school the next day. After we hung up I yawned, my eyelids feeling heavy. Part of me wanted to remain on the floor and fall asleep right where I was, but I knew I should get up, wash my face and curl up under the warm covers.

"Too cold," I mumbled.

A second later, I felt a warm sensation, almost as if someone was lowering a blanket onto me.

"Charlotte." It was just a whisper, faint and far away. I was drifting in that hazy space between asleep and awake, but I felt tugged toward sleep and had the sense that I was sinking slowly. I felt cool grass beneath me, and I could smell jasmine in the air. I was back at the park in Charleston where Annalise and I had eaten lunch a few weeks before, near the same tree where the dark-haired girl in my dreams liked to read. I felt as if I was waiting for the girl to arrive. In fact, I felt sure that she would arrive at any moment, that I should stay exactly where I was.

"Charlotte?"

I opened my eyes. Mom was standing over me, looking down. I sat up, confused.

"I fell asleep," I mumbled.

"You were talking." Mom reached down and helped pull me up.

"What did I say?"

"I'm not sure. It was more like whispering." Mom cocked her head to one side. "You okay?"

"Just tired. I'm going to bed now." I went to the bathroom and brushed my teeth. When I returned, Mom had picked up the last of my dirty clothes, including Annalise's pink sweater.

"I'll take these downstairs for you," she said. She leaned over and kissed my forehead. "Sleep well. See you in the morning."

I got into bed and fell asleep almost immediately. It was a hard and dreamless sleep, and when I woke up early the next morning, I felt more rested than I had in weeks. I had the vague impression that something odd had occurred the night before, but I couldn't put my finger on it. Had I been dreaming?

As I showered, I decided that everything was fine. I'd experienced some strange sensations, but I was living in a new place and that was bound to happen. Maybe I was just extra sensitive to temperature in the South. Whatever was happening, it wasn't that big of a deal. I wouldn't let myself dwell on it. Besides, I had more important things to focus on.

It was time to introduce Charlotte Silver, Average Ordinary Girl, to the rest of the senior class.

five

Avery wasn't kidding when she said seven-thirty sharp. I was just peeling a banana when I heard two quick honks of a car in the driveway. I glanced at the kitchen clock: 7:29.

"That's my cue," I said to Mom. She was still in her bathrobe, sitting at the kitchen counter and sipping a cup of coffee.

"Good luck, hon. Have a great day."

I gathered up my backpack and left the house just as Avery honked once more. I slid into the passenger seat and smiled.

"A little impatient, aren't we?"

She pulled out of the driveway. "Sorry. I hate being late, is all."

I settled into my seat. "We've got plenty of time."

My parents and I had driven past the school once, and it was no more than ten minutes from our house. Even if there was morning traffic, we would get to school with about half an hour to spare.

"You still need to pick up your schedule," Avery reminded

me. She had received hers in the mail the week before, but since I registered so late, I had to stop by the main office to pick up mine.

Avery chatted about some of her friends. "They're really nice," she said. "You'll like them."

"Are they all cheerleaders?"

She glanced at me. "Yes. But don't worry. We're not cliquey or snobby or anything. You'll fit right in."

"So they won't try to recruit me? I'm highly uncoordinated. I can barely clap in rhythm."

Avery grinned. "You may want to work on that. But no recruiting, I promise. We will not try to bring you over to the dark side."

I noticed that, once again, we were taking a shortcut that was anything but short. In fact, it seemed like Avery never took the main road if she could avoid it, even if it meant driving miles out of her way. I asked her about it once after we took the long way to pick up medicine from Dante's vet.

"I don't like heavy traffic," she had said with a shrug. "And I want to be careful with my new car."

We arrived at school, and Avery turned into the section reserved for seniors. About half a dozen girls stood in one corner. When they saw Avery's car, they all waved happily, then parted like a wave. They had been blocking off a specific space, I realized, to make sure that no one else could park there.

We stepped out of the car and were greeted by a chorus of hellos. Some of the girls offered Avery quick hugs. They complimented her clothes and said how great it was to see her. I hung back, waiting to be introduced.

"This is Charlotte," Avery said finally. "She just moved here from Charleston."

The girls smiled and looked at me closely. I smiled in return, suddenly self-conscious. They were sizing me up, I thought, judging whether or not I would be accepted into their circle. I was sure Avery had told them about me, but how much?

"Do you cheer?" asked one. I wasn't sure who had spoken. All the girls had long, light-colored hair and perfect tans.

"Uh, no. Sorry, I don't cheer."

Avery laughed. "But we'll overlook that one little personality flaw, won't we?" she asked, and the other girls giggled at the joke.

"Any friend of Avery's is a friend of ours," said a girl to my left, and the others nodded and murmured their agreement. I relaxed a little. Avery suggested we go to the main office to pick up my class schedule, and we all walked as one big group across the parking lot and into the school.

We attracted more than a little attention as we made our way through the wide, crowded hallways. The girls pointed out to me where the cafeteria was and chatted about who they had for English and math. When we got to the office, they formed a semicircle behind me as I waited for the secretary to locate my schedule.

"Your locker number and combination are here," said the frowning woman as she pointed to the bottom of my schedule. Then she noticed Avery, and something in her face softened.

"How are you, dear?" she asked. Genuine concern filled her voice.

"Fine, thanks," Avery replied brightly. Then she nudged me and we left.

The girls passed around my schedule, comparing it with their own. "She's in B lunch!" exclaimed one.

Avery smiled. "That means we all have lunch together."

When we reached the senior hallway, Avery checked my locker number. "Callie, would you mind showing Charlotte to her locker?"

The tallest girl in the group reached for my schedule. She looked down at the number, then up at Avery. Something passed between them, but I wasn't sure what it was. "Of course," she said. "We'll catch up with you later."

Avery and the other girls went in one direction while Callie and I went in the other. "We have the same first period," Callie said happily. "So we can walk to class together."

She stopped at the last locker before the drinking fountain. "Here it is."

"Thanks." I tried the combination, but it didn't work.

"Allow me." Callie twirled the lock. This time, the door popped open. I unzipped my backpack and pulled out a notebook and my purse.

"We haven't seen much of Avery this summer," Callie said. "How's she doing?"

I hung my backpack on a hook. "She's good. She's been helping me unpack and get settled in and everything."

"That's nice." Callie looked around, then lowered her voice. "Has she talked to you about, you know, stuff?"

I looked at her. "What kind of stuff?"

Callie hesitated. "Nothing, nothing." She began to lean against the locker next to mine, but as soon as her back touched it, she flinched like she'd been burned.

"You okay?"

Callie looked around to see if anyone had noticed her strange reaction. "I'm fine. Sorry—must have lost my balance for a second. You ready?"

I shut my locker. "Lead the way."

Our first class of the day was British Lit with Dr. Larsen,

a severe-looking older woman with a passion for Yeats and a strict no-pencil policy.

"If it is not written in ink, I will not read it," she announced, handing out the syllabus. "And I do not mean purple ink, or red or glitter-infused chartreuse. Black or blue only. Preferably black."

I checked my pen supply. I had brought the ones Annalise put in my care package, and they were all bright, unacceptable colors. Callie was sitting across from me. She saw me looking through my pens and handed me a black one.

"Thanks," I whispered.

"Welcome to Lincoln High," she whispered back.

We were opening our textbooks when a guy with shaggy brown hair limped into the room. Dr. Larsen stopped in the middle of warning us about the severe consequences of blemishing the pages of her textbooks with so much as a squiggly line and looked at him.

"Mr. James. How good of you to join us."

He shrugged and handed her a tardy slip. The entire classroom watched as he shuffled to the back of the room and slid into an empty desk. I gave him a quick once-over and decided he was cute but too disheveled, like he'd just rolled out of bed before coming to school. I returned to my book, but when I glanced over at Callie, she was watching the guy intensely. A few other kids were staring, too, but the guy looked straight ahead and didn't acknowledge anyone.

The rest of the day was a slow, boring exercise in repetition: we listened to the same lectures about classroom behavior, read the same student handbook pages covering schoolwide rules, and wrote our names over and over on emergency contact cards and book forms and "I understand all the rules as they have been explained to me" contracts. I had lunch with the girls, who shared horror stories about Dr. Larsen ("too strict"), complained about the cafeteria food ("too salty") and gossiped about the guys ("too immature").

At one point, the noise of the cafeteria decreased notice-ably, as if most people had stopped talking at the same time. I looked around. The guy from first period had entered, limping slowly past the tables. The sudden silence was soon replaced with loud whispers.

"Who is that?" I asked.

The girls exchanged glances. "Jared James," Callie said fi-nally. "He's a loser."

"I can't believe they even let him back in here after last year," said another.

I wanted to ask about what had happened to make Jared James such an obvious outcast, but Avery cleared her throat. "Let's not discuss it, okay? He's not worth it."

Callie nodded. "You're right. We won't even say his name."

Everyone agreed. For a moment, it felt tense, then Avery laughed. "Did I tell you guys about the time Harris Abbott stole all of Doc Larsen's pens and replaced them with pencils?"

The conversation returned to lighter, more comfortable ground, and while everyone tried to make me feel as if I was a part of the group, it was odd not knowing what they knew. I looked across the room. Jared was sitting by himself at an empty table. There had been a loud group of people eating there minutes earlier. They must have left when Jared sat down with his lunch, I realized.

I watched Jared unwrap a sandwich. He wasn't awkward or grotesque. If anything, he looked athletic, like a football player, maybe. And he was definitely attractive, in a rugged, unkempt kind of way. The only thing off about him was the limp, and I didn't believe that anyone was ostracizing him because of that, specifically. I hoped that Avery would tell me more later, when there weren't so many people around.

Finally it was the last period of the day, which was reserved for electives. Most of the girls had yearbook, including Avery. I had not been so lucky.

"AV Club?" Callie frowned. "There's got to be a way to get you out of that."

"Yearbook was my first choice," I said. "Guess it was full."

"Charlotte's parents make documentary films," Avery said. "So it should be an easy A." She turned to me. "AV is not ideal, but the teacher's nice. Just avoid Bliss Reynolds. She's a senior with a diva complex."

"And if she hassles you too much, let us know," Callie added.

Avery patted my shoulder. "See you after school. Think about it—freedom is just fifty minutes away."

I smiled and followed her directions to the north hallway. The AV room shared a small, dark corner next to the band room. The Nerd Nest, Callie had joked at lunch. I passed a room where someone was lightly tapping a snare drum, and opened the wide door of the AV room, walking right into utter chaos.

"The lights!" a girl was screeching. "Noah, you have to do something about those lights!"

"No, Alex has to do something about the lights. I'm supposed to fix the camera."

"The camera doesn't matter if the lights are too dim, brainiac."

I spotted a guy bent over a tripod camera, examining the cables.

"Check the output," I said.

He looked up, and I was surprised by how perfectly green his eyes were. I wondered if he wore colored contacts. "Which one is the output?"

I knelt down next to him and located the cable. "Should be this one."

A light came on, and the guy smiled. "It worked! Thanks."

"No problem."

He wiped his hand on his pants and offered it to me. "I'm Noah."

I shook his hand. "Charlotte."

I looked around the room. A long table was set up at the front, with a white backdrop hanging behind it and bright lights secured above it. Three ancient cameras were pointing toward the table.

"You're in the wrong room, sweetheart."

A girl dressed in lavender jeans and a matching short-sleeved shirt was standing in front of me, her hands on her hips. "Hello? Did you hear me? I said you're in the wrong room."

I was confused. "This is AV, right?"

The teacher walked into the room then, clapping his hands together and trying to get everyone's attention. "Okay, folks! Let's gather round! Lots to do and not a lot of time!"

"Mr. Morley, I absolutely refuse to coanchor the school news," announced the girl. "I'm a senior!"

"Bliss, calm down. Who said you were coanchoring?"

A small group of kids had gathered around Mr. Morley. They were all guys, and most of them appeared to be freshmen. Some of them looked so young they could have been middle schoolers.

Bliss pointed at me, and I noticed that even her nails were painted a light shade of purple. "Who is *that?*"

"My name is Charlotte," I said, ignoring Bliss and looking directly at Mr. Morley. "I'm new here."

"Well, welcome, Charlotte. Do you have any experience with camera work?"

"Yes." I glanced at Bliss. "My parents make documentary films. I usually help them with sound."

Mr. Morley beamed. "Excellent! Just what we need."

"As long as she stays behind the camera," Bliss muttered.

The goal of the class, Mr. Morley explained, was to produce a five-minute news show each day that would be aired the next morning in homeroom. What it boiled down to was Bliss reading the announcements and game scores for the week. We also had to sign up to film at least two sports events each semester. If we finished early, the class became a study hall. It wasn't a big deal—except to Bliss Reynolds, apparently. She cornered me just after the final bell rang.

"If you're waiting for me to miss a class so you can take over, don't bother," she said. "I don't take sick days."

"How about mental health days?" I asked. "I think you could use one."

I wasn't sure what had possessed me to blurt out something so harsh, but my accumulated experiences at six different high schools had taught me one social truth: let someone treat you badly once, and they'll keep doing it day after day. Show people you're not a doormat, and they'll look for someone else to step on. I hoped my comeback would effectively keep Bliss off my back.

Her eyes widened with what I could only interpret as rage. "If you think that I would allow some no-name newcomer to sweep in here and steal my job—"

"Hello, Bliss." Avery and Callie were standing behind me, smiling sweetly. Bliss stood frozen in place, her mouth still open.

"Charlotte? Ready to go?" Avery was staring hard at Bliss.

"Absolutely. See you later, Bliss."

It felt strangely powerful to turn my back on Bliss and walk away with my new friends.

"What was her problem?" Callie asked.

"She thinks I'm after her news-anchoring job," I said. "Personally, I prefer to stay behind the camera, so she's got nothing to worry about."

"Don't let her know that," Avery advised. "Keep her guessing."

"She seemed a little intimidated by you guys," I said, choosing my words carefully.

Callie laughed. "I doubt it. We've known her forever."

Avery stopped just before we reached my locker. "Bliss just feels guilty, is all. She wrote a story for the student paper last year, and she got her facts all wrong and upset a lot of people."

"Oh. What was the story about?"

"Something she knew nothing about," Callie muttered.

Avery shot Callie a glance. "It was about the cheerleaders," she said. "I need to stop at my locker. I'll meet you guys outside."

My backpack weighed about a hundred pounds after I filled it with all the books I needed. "I can't believe I have so much homework," I complained.

Callie laughed. "The teachers always start off hard. It'll get better."

As we were walking out to the parking lot, I remembered that I left my English notebook behind.

"Tell Avery I'll be there in a minute." I dropped my backpack to the sidewalk, where it landed with a heavy thump.

I walked quickly, not wanting to make Avery wait. As I turned the corner into the senior hallway, I spotted a guy at the drinking fountain next to my locker. It was Jared. He looked up as I approached.

"Hey."

I nodded and began turning the lock. I tried opening the door, but it wouldn't budge.

"Need help?"

He's a loser, the girls had warned me. Nothing about him struck me as all that terrible, though. His voice was soft, and his limp made him seem, well, vulnerable.

"I can do it," I said. "It's been sticking all day."

Jared took an awkward step forward. "Make sure you turn it all the way around first," he said. "That seems to help."

"I'll do that." I gave him a quick smile and tried again. This time, it opened. "It worked," I said, pulling my notebook off the shelf. "Thanks."

When I shut the door and looked over at the drinking fountain, he was gone. I returned to the parking lot. Avery was in her car and my backpack was already inside.

"Ready?"

I thought about telling her that I'd run into Jared, but then decided against it. He'd only spoken a few words to me, so it wasn't a big deal, and I didn't want to upset her. *We won't even say his name,* Callie had decided at lunch. I had agreed to that. I had also decided that I needed to know more.

As Avery pulled out of the parking lot and headed toward our neighborhood, I resolved to find a way to get the whole story from her. Whatever Jared had done, it couldn't be too awful, could it? He was still in school, so it wasn't like he'd been expelled or arrested or anything. Of course, people got away with terrible things all the time. Maybe that's why everyone hated him.

"So what did you think of Lincoln High?" Avery asked as she turned away from the main road.

"It's got a lot going on," I replied.

six

It was nighttime and I was standing outside in an unfamiliar place, a slender sliver of moon shining overhead. Tall tombstones dotted the ground. There was something strange about them. A light breeze passed, rippling the stones. I realized they weren't graves at all but homemade tents constructed of pale sheets. This wasn't a cemetery—it was a park.

The dark-haired girl emerged from one of the tents. She was wearing a pink dress that flowed to her ankles. Her black hair was pulled into a long braid, and for a second she reminded me of Annalise, dressed in an old-fashioned costume for one of my parents' films. This wasn't a costume, though—she was clad in the clothes of her time, which I guessed was at least a hundred years ago.

I watched as the girl crept past the other tents. Somewhere, a baby cried softly. The girl hesitated. She looked around, then continued walking quickly. When she reached the edge of the park, she turned around. "Goodbye," she whispered, and I thought her voice sounded exactly like my own. The girl hurried off into the darkness, away from the park, away from the tents, away from everything.

The dream was still clear in my mind as I walked to Avery's house. It was the first weekend of September, and my parents had gone to Charleston that morning to visit Annalise. They wouldn't be back until after dinner, so Avery invited me over to help her brainstorm ideas for Homecoming.

"I'm leading the committee," she'd told me the night before. "And I want to present some fantastic ideas before our big meeting next week."

"I don't know how I can help," I'd told her. "I don't have a lot of experience with Homecoming."

"Perfect," Avery had replied. "You'll give me a fresh perspective."

My perspective was anything but fresh as I knocked on her door. I was strangely groggy, even though I'd had more than enough sleep. The dream was all I could think about. It had felt so real, like I was standing there with the girl, watching events unfold from just a few steps away.

Avery opened the door. She was cradling Dante in her arms. As soon as the little dog saw me, he whimpered, but Avery didn't seem to notice. "You're here! Excellent. Let's go up to my room."

I had seen Avery's bedroom before—in the pages of a magazine. Pale pink walls were accented by a black chair rail and patterned throw pillows. Everything was coordinated, from the curtains to the framed pictures to the white bowl of rose buds on her nightstand.

"Wow," I breathed. The air held the soft scent of roses. My bare, beige room looked like a utility closet in comparison.

"Do you like it? It's supposed to be 'modern tranquil.' That's what my mom's designer said, at least."

"It's gorgeous," I said, taking it all in.

I'd known Avery for nearly a month, and it was the first time I'd been inside her house, which was lovely and organized and had a living room that was actually used as, well, a living room.

Avery gently placed Dante on a pink silk pillow and sat cross-legged on her bed while I walked over to her dresser, where a cluster of pictures sat in identical black frames.

"Is this Adam?" I held up a picture of her standing close to a tall guy with a wide, toothy smile. He was wearing a tux and Avery was dressed in a sapphire-blue gown.

"That was from last year's prom."

Some of the pictures were of Avery with Dante and a few were shots of Dante alone, but most of them featured Avery with Adam. I picked up another one of the two of them. She was in her cheerleading uniform while he was dressed in a football uniform. They had their arms around each other and were smiling. Behind them I could see the field and the blurry figures of people wandering around after a game.

"How long have you dated?" I asked.

"We met at Homecoming my freshman year. After that we were kind of inseparable."

I picked up a picture that appeared to be Adam's senior photo. He had light brown hair and even lighter brown eyes. "He's hot."

Avery giggled. "I think so."

I remembered Callie asking me if Avery had talked to me about "stuff." This must be what she meant, I thought. Her long-term boyfriend had graduated and gone off to college, leaving her behind.

"I bet you miss him."

"I do." Her voice was quieter. "I talk to him every day, but still. It's hard." She looked down at her hands, and I thought for a moment that she was going to cry. But then she looked up, smiling. "Want to see my yearbooks?"

"Absolutely."

She went to a shelf and pulled two heavy books from it. We both sat on her bed. Dante growled in his sleep when I sat down but remained curled up on his pillow. Avery began with her freshman year, pointing out pictures of her and Adam. There were tons of them.

"I can't believe how young we look!" She giggled.

"I know. It's like in my AV class. All the boys look like *boys*."

I had spent the first week of school carefully avoiding Bliss Reynolds. It wasn't too difficult because she usually left at the beginning of class with an obedient camera guy in tow. It was difficult for me to comprehend why she was so hostile toward me, but her angry glares and impatient sighs any time we came within a few feet of one another told me that she definitely considered me an enemy. We were the only girls in the class. Callie told me that Bliss had basically threatened any girl who had expressed an interest in AV with her unbridled wrath. Did she really believe that I was a threat? And if so, a threat to what? AV class couldn't possibly mean that much to someone. It was a high school elective, not a life-altering career move.

After combing through the freshman yearbook, Avery moved on to her sophomore edition. Signatures crammed the front pages—it seemed as if everyone in the school had signed her book. When she turned to the sports section, I noticed a picture of Adam with his arm draped around another guy. It didn't register at first, but then I realized the other person was Jared. Avery turned the page quickly, but I knew she had seen it. Now was my chance, I thought. Maybe I could finally get some answers.

"So what's the story with Jared?" I asked.

"Story?" Avery concentrated on the glossy black-and-white pages of the yearbook.

"Avery, please. Everyone but me knows some deep dark secret about him. It's weird. And no one will tell me anything."

"That's because I told them not to."

I was taken aback. "Why?"

She looked at me. "They think they know the whole story, but they don't. And I didn't want you to hear bits and pieces, some of it true and some of it not. If you really need to know, I'll tell you." She closed the yearbook. "But, Charlotte, I'm only doing this once. I don't want to talk about it again—ever. Okay?"

I nodded. Part of me was relieved to finally get the information I wanted, but part of me was scared of what Avery was about to tell me.

"Adam and Jared were best friends," she began. "More like brothers, really. They grew up together."

Avery said that Jared wasn't thrilled when his best friend began devoting so much time to her, but he learned to live with it. The three of them often went to movies together or hung out. Sometimes Jared brought a date, but he was never with one girl for very long. Avery had even tried to fix him up with Callie during their sophomore year, but the two dated for less than a month. Callie complained that Jared never wanted to do anything unless it was with Avery and Adam.

Things began to change when Adam became a senior. "He was so busy with college applications and school and being with me," Avery said. "Jared started getting left out of things. He was angry."

Adam spent Christmas in Rome with his family. While he was gone, Avery and Jared went to a party together. "Long story short, he kissed me," Avery said, sighing. "He'd been drinking and he was lonely, I guess. I told him to get a grip and sober up, but he was out of his mind. He kept coming on to me in front of everyone. It was crazy."

When Adam returned from Rome, he heard rumors that Avery and Jared had hooked up. He confronted them, the truth came out, and Adam never trusted Jared again.

"I think Jared felt betrayed," Avery said. "He thought that Adam had taken my side over his, but there wasn't a choice, really. Jared crossed a line."

"What happened to him?" I asked. "How did he get the limp? Why won't anyone go near him?" I knew there was more to the story. An entire school did not turn against someone just because he kissed the wrong girl.

"There was an accident," Avery said softly. "Jared got into a fight with Adam after a party. He was driving too fast and he hit a telephone pole. It messed up his leg." She ran her hand across the cover of the yearbook. "After that, he stopped talking to anyone. Sometimes he would punch a locker or a wall. He makes people nervous, like he might explode at any second."

"That's why people avoid him? They're afraid he might go crazy?"

Avery got up and put the yearbooks away. I realized that we hadn't looked through last year's book, and when I glanced at the neatly organized bookshelf, I saw that there was no space for it.

"They're afraid he *has* gone crazy," she said. "He's not the same. He's dangerous."

"Dangerous how?" There was something she wasn't telling me. *I can't believe they even let him back in here after last year,* someone had commented on the first day of school. What had Jared done?

Avery's back was to me as she stood in front of her bookshelf. "He's dangerous because he's unpredictable." She turned around, and I could see that her eyes were red. "I can't talk about this anymore."

I nodded. "I'm sorry if this is painful for you. I didn't mean to pry."

She wiped her eyes. "It's not you. I'm just trying to forget the bad stuff and hang on to the good stuff, you know? And sometimes seeing Jared makes that hard to do."

I suspected that she was leaving out details, things she felt guilty about. Maybe the incident with Jared had gone further than just a drunken kiss at a party. Whatever she wasn't saying, I let it go. Avery had told me enough and I trusted her judgment. She was my friend, and that was all that mattered.

We spent the rest of the day working on Homecoming themes. We came up with a few good ideas and a few backup plans. Avery was leaning toward "Masquerade Ball" because Homecoming fell on the day after Halloween and she wanted something festive yet elegant.

"Not like last year," she said. "It was a retro, 1980s theme. Basically it was just an excuse for everyone to dress like the extras in a Madonna video. I want to step it up this year."

I called home around eight that night to see if my parents had gotten back from Charleston, but there was no answer.

"You can stay here as long as you like," Avery offered.

"Thanks. I'll try again later."

We talked about school for a while, and Avery told me that cheerleading practice would soon be taking up more of her time. "I won't be able to give you a ride home after school most days," she said.

"No problem," I assured her. "I'll take the bus."

"The bus?" She pretended to shudder. "You can go to the library or something and I can take you home after practice is over."

"I might do that. We'll see." I didn't want Avery to feel as if she was obligated to serve as my chauffeur, or worse, that I had nothing better to do than read in the library while she went to practice.

An hour later, I decided to go home. Avery's mom made me promise to call once I'd gotten there, which I thought was odd because I lived just up the hill. I knew she was watching me from the window as I made the short walk to my house. When I reached the front door, I flipped on the porch light. Sure enough, their front light turned off.

Inside my house it was completely dark. I reached for the light switch, sliding my hands across the wall. But just as I was about to flick it on, I heard a noise upstairs.

Footsteps.

I froze, my hand on the wall, and listened. Someone was definitely upstairs. I reached into my pocket for my cell phone and took a step back toward the front door. I kept my eyes on the stairs and my hand on the cell phone. A light flashed across the hallway.

"Over here," a voice said. "I'm getting something."

It was Shane. I realized I had been holding my breath, and I let it out, relieved, and ran up the stairs. The door to my room was open, and as I stood in the doorway I could see

Shane and my parents standing near my bed, looking down at something.

"What's going on in here?" I demanded. Everyone jumped.

"Charlotte, you startled us!" Mom exclaimed.

I turned on the light to my room and gasped. My parents had all of their equipment out—the ion meters and recorders and even the thermal camera. They brought the thermal along only if they felt confident that it would capture something on-screen. Something paranormal.

"Seriously," I said. "What's going on?"

Shane coughed. My parents looked at each other. Dad set the thermal reader down on my bed.

"We need to talk," he said.

Mom walked over to me. "Let's go downstairs."

She put one arm around my shoulder and ushered me out of my room. Dad was right behind us. "It's time we showed you something."

As we headed toward the living room, I couldn't help feeling dread. It was as if I was being led to my own beheading.

Dad sat at one of the long tables and turned on a video screen. I immediately recognized the Courtyard Café in Charleston. Annalise and I were standing in the middle of the room and she was speaking. "Hello? Do you remember me? I was here last month. I felt—something. Was it you? Is someone here?" Dad fast forwarded the tape. I could see myself leaning toward Annalise and whispering in her ear. A second later, something happened. Dad froze the screen.

"Do you see those white shapes?" he asked.

I sucked in my breath. "What is it?"

Mom shook her head. "We're not sure yet. But, Charlotte, whatever they are, it appears that they followed us here."

"What do you mean? What are you talking about?"

Shane came downstairs. "Got something!"

Dad turned to me. "We think something powerful was triggered back in Charleston. We're getting readings stronger than anything we've ever recorded."

My legs felt shaky and I gripped the back of Dad's chair. The still images on the screen stared back at me. "Do you know what caused it?" I asked. No one said anything. I looked at Mom. "What triggered it?"

"You did," she said gently. "We think you're the trigger."

seven

I'd never felt so far from normal. Staring at the pale images frozen on the screen, I was overwhelmed by the notion that normal was a kind of place where other people lived but I had never even visited.

"What are they?" I asked for the third time.

Shane was hooking up the EVP readings. Mom and Dad sat at each side of me. "We think we have two distinct energies here," Dad said. He pointed to a large mass of white on the screen. "We've connected this one with a male voice and this smaller one with a female voice."

The shapes on the screen did not look like people, exactly, but they were tall and thin, like pillars, and they hovered a foot off the ground, staying close to my side for several frames.

"So you're saying that I did something that brought out two ghosts, and these ghosts are now following me around?"

"Not ghosts, honey. Energy," Dad corrected.

"White, wispy shapes that float around are ghosts," I said angrily. "I don't want to hear about harmless energy."

Dad frowned but said nothing.

Shane pulled up the EVP screen. "Here we go," he said, increasing the volume. At first, all I could hear was static. But the monitor showed spikes in noise, and when the recording reached those points, there was an audible whispering sound.

"Isolate it," Dad instructed, and Shane clicked on the sound.

"I see her," a man's voice whispered.

A chill spread through me. Shane played it again. Never had three little words terrified me so much.

I see her.

I felt numb. "When was this recorded?"

"Just a few minutes ago, when you were standing in the doorway," Shane said. He seemed excited, like he'd hit the paranormal jackpot. He lived for this stuff, but he could return to his safe little apartment after finding something freaky. I wasn't so lucky. How was I going to sleep in my room when I knew that I was sharing it with disembodied stalkers?

"What kind of things have you experienced since we've lived here?" Mom asked. "I remember you mentioned a strange dream once. Was that right after we moved in?"

I realized she was using her professional voice, the one she used when she interviewed "clients." I felt a fresh flash of anger—I wasn't a client, I was her daughter.

"Yes, I've had a few strange dreams. And I've felt some cold spots. Sometimes, I think I hear whispers." I kept my voice calm and matter-of-fact. I knew my parents didn't trust overly emotional people.

"What do you remember about your dreams?"

"There's always the same girl in them," I said. "And they

seem to take place a hundred years ago. Maybe more than a hundred years."

Dad and Shane were still staring at the computer screen and mumbling things to one another. I stood up.

"I can't stay here," I announced. "I'm going to Avery's."

Mom followed me up the stairs to my room. I opened my dresser and pulled out some clothes, tossing them onto the bed.

"How long have you known?" I asked her.

She sat on the bed and began folding my crumpled shirts. "We finally figured it out today. At first, we thought it was connected to Annalise. The EVPs we captured mentioned a female. We just assumed…"

I slammed a drawer shut. "You just assumed what?"

Mom frowned. "You know that Annalise has always been more sensitive to energy than you. She has great intuition and the ability to elicit a response. You're different."

"Different? Is that your way of saying that I'm basically useless to your research?" Mom flinched, and even I was surprised at the venom in my voice. I wasn't sure if I was revealing my true feelings or simply releasing some of my anger and fear.

Mom reached for my hand. "Your father and I have never, ever seen you as anything but a vital and essential part of this family and our team."

I let her pull me into a hug. "I know." After a moment I pulled away. "So you're sure these things are focused on me?"

"Unfortunately, yes." Mom gathered up my clothes into a little pile. "When we visited Annalise today, she was fine. She hasn't felt anything at all strange since we left. So we went back over our footage and realized we had been looking at it all wrong."

I grabbed a duffel bag from my closet. "I thought only buildings were supposed to be haunted. I thought ghosts stayed put, not followed people around."

I knew Mom hated the word "ghosts," but I didn't care. As far as I was concerned, this was her fault. Her and Dad's. They exposed me to something strange and creepy, and now they needed to find a way to stop it.

"We'll figure this out," Mom said. "Charlotte, I promise you. Once we identify the trigger, we can stop it."

"You said I was the trigger."

Mom placed my clothes in the duffel bag. "Yes, but it could be more specific than that. It could be something you did, something you said. We're reviewing all the tapes."

I remembered walking in the living room days earlier and the way they'd tried to keep me from hearing something. "There was another EVP, wasn't there? One from Charleston?"

"Yes." Mom was being careful not to make eye contact with me. She focused instead on arranging the clothes in my bag.

"I want to hear it."

"Okay."

I was expecting more resistance from her, but she must have heard the determination in my voice. We returned downstairs and Mom asked Shane to pull up the file. I slipped on a pair of headphones. Shane pushed a button and I heard the familiar buzz of static.

"Her," a low, male voice whispered.

"Daughter," a female voice said. The woman's voice was slightly clearer and louder.

I took off the headphones. "They think I'm their daughter?"

"We've got Annalise researching the restaurant," Dad said.

"She's trying to figure out who the couple may be, if they had a daughter, when they died, that kind of thing."

Shane tapped a pencil against the table, something he always did when he was thinking. "I'm trying to find a connection between your two visits," he said. "Something that's the same both times." He squinted at the screen, and I followed his gaze. I had a nagging sense that I knew the answer.

"I'll think about it," I told them. "But for now, I'm going to Avery's. I'll be back tomorrow." I paused. "You don't think they're following me outside of my bedroom, do you?"

"That never happens," Dad said. "Energy manifests itself in one place at a time." He sounded confident, but I wondered if he was just saying that so I wouldn't worry too much. I decided to believe him, mainly because I wanted to. He gave me a hug, and Mom walked with me out of the house. She stood on the porch, watching to make sure I made it safely down the street. When I reached Avery's door, I turned and waved. I saw my mom, illuminated by the porch light and I was filled with an inexplicable sadness. I felt like I was waving goodbye, and the sensation was so strong and heavy and real that when Avery opened the door, I burst out crying.

"What's wrong?" she asked, pulling me inside.

"Almost everything," I sobbed.

My official excuse for staying with Avery was that I was having "problems at home," which was basically true. Having ghosts (I refused to call them "energy") occupying your bedroom is, indeed, a problem, although not one that is easily explained. Avery and her mom didn't pester me with questions, which I appreciated.

"I want you to know that if you ever feel like talking about it, I'm here," Avery told me as she set up a sleeping bag on her floor. "No pressure, but if you need someone to listen, day or night, you've got me."

It was such a sincere and thoughtful offer, and the crushing sense of desolation I'd experienced earlier had not faded, that I almost spilled my secret right then and there. Instead, I held back. I didn't know how she would react, and I didn't want to risk losing her friendship.

"You're helping me more than you know," I told her. "Thanks for letting me stay here."

"Any time," she responded. I think Avery assumed that I was having problems with my parents, that maybe they were going to be separating or something. I knew that Avery's parents had divorced when she was three, and that her dad lived across the country.

"I see him around holidays and a week during the summer," she'd told me. "It's not a big deal. It's always been like this, so I can't really miss what I never had."

I remembered being in the sixth grade and realizing that out of everyone in my class, I was the only one whose parents were still married. At the time, I thought divorce was the natural progression of things. I kept waiting for my parents to announce they were splitting up. For a while, it made me feel left out a little, like all the other kids had gone through some important rite of passage that I hadn't. It was a long time before I figured out that I was lucky.

I spent the next three nights sleeping on Avery's floor. She offered me her bed, but I felt bad enough for taking over half her room, so I insisted that the sleeping bag was comfortable and that I actually enjoyed it.

During my second night I perused Avery's bookshelf while she downloaded songs onto her MP3 player. She mainly owned classic paperbacks required for summer reading, but one book caught my eye and I pulled it from the shelf. *Greetings from Beyond the Grave* read the gold-embossed title. I knew the author because my dad was one of his loudest critics. He said August Zelden was a phony, someone who preyed on grieving people by giving them false hope that their loved ones were trying to send them messages after death.

"It was a gift."

I looked up. Avery was smiling at me. "Someone gave it to me. I don't know why I kept it."

"I've seen Zelden on TV," I said, turning the book over in my hands. The back cover showed a picture of the author, a middle-aged man with a serene smile. "He's very convincing."

"Do you believe in it?"

"In this? No."

Avery came over and sat down on the floor next to me. "Not even a little bit?"

I shrugged. "I always wondered why, if someone could talk to spirits, they never asked the really obvious questions. Like, what it's like over there, or what exactly happens after you die? Instead, you just hear that they want to wish people well and remind them to get a checkup."

"What about ghosts? Do you believe in those?"

"Ghosts are different. You can see them or hear them or track them in some way. And yes, I believe they exist."

Avery nodded. "So do I. But I've never seen one."

I had, but I didn't tell her that. Instead, I asked why she believed in something she'd never seen. She thought for a moment before answering.

"I guess it's because so many other people swear they've seen one. I mean, there've been ghost stories for thousands of years, right? They have to be based on *something*."

"You're right," I said. "They must be based on something."

I had often thought that my parents too easily dismissed some of their findings. They wanted tangible evidence to examine, and I understood that, but their theories about energy didn't leave a lot of room for the things that couldn't be caught on their high-tech devices, such as the creepy feelings that could fill an empty room, the sense that *something* was watching you. I had years of experience wandering around abandoned asylums and vacant prisons and deserted houses. Those experiences had taught me the difference between a place that was spooky yet harmless and one that held something more. I could tell within ten seconds of walking into a place if we were going to get readings on the equipment, and I wasn't as sensitive as Annalise, who knew the instant we pulled in front of a location if there was energy present.

Now there was energy present in my new room, in my new house. The thought made it difficult for me to fall asleep at night. I would close my eyes and listen to the sounds around me, the slow rhythm of Avery's breathing, Dante's weird, light snoring and the steady ticking of the clock on the dresser. Sometimes I could hear distant traffic or bullfrogs singing outside. I tried to make my mind blank by picturing a vast space of pure, endless black, but my thoughts kept tumbling back to what I had seen on the monitor, the ghostly figures floating next to me.

My parents had always found it amusing that people took hauntings personally, as if they had been chosen to experience something. They believed that some people were simply more sensitive to energy than others, and it was all a matter of being in the right place at the right time. Or the wrong place at the wrong time, depending on how you looked at it. They would interview people who were freaked out because they thought a ghost was after them for some reason. "Nothing is after you," Mom and Dad would say. "It really has nothing to do with you."

I repeated those lines to myself as I tried to fall asleep. *Nothing is after you. It really has nothing to do with you.* But I don't think even my parents believed that. Whatever this was, it had everything to do with me.

eight

Life doesn't stop just because you're being stalked by ghosts. It doesn't even slow down. And if I thought for a second my parents would ease up and maybe let me drive their car or hang out later than usual, I was sadly mistaken.

After spending three nights at Avery's, my parents decided that it was time I came home. They claimed to "have a handle on things." I thought they were just worried that Avery and her mom might think the problems at home were worse than they actually were and they would be labeled bad parents. I agreed to return, but I didn't want to sleep in my bedroom. Instead, I slept on the couch in our dining room. I felt more comfortable downstairs, but I couldn't escape the sense that I was being observed. I would pull a blanket over my head and convince myself that paranormal energy couldn't see through flannel, but it was taking me longer and longer each night to fall asleep. My only consolation was that I hadn't had a dream about the dark-haired girl for a while. Those dreams hadn't been bad, exactly, just strange, and I'd had enough strange in the past week to last me a lifetime.

"We'll get this figured out," Dad reassured me. "We're working on it."

As the days passed and we settled into September, I found myself looking forward to school each day. I had a nice routine established: Avery picked me up at seven-thirty, and we met the other girls in the parking lot before walking to our lockers. At lunch, I sat with a large, loud group, and I stayed after school for an hour while Avery went to cheerleading practice. Usually I finished my homework in the library, but sometimes Mr. Morley asked me to edit footage for the school news. This meant that I spent the hour watching Bliss Reynolds on a screen interviewing people in a perky-yet-serious voice that I found irritating after about five minutes.

"She's truly annoying," I mumbled once as I viewed the day's footage with Noah. On the screen, Bliss was standing in front of a small tree and giving a particularly impassioned speech about the school needing to form more of an environmental conscience.

"She's not so bad," Noah said. "She's just really focused. Believe me, she's a lot better than the girl we had last year."

"So Bliss wasn't the only girl in class last year?"

Noah shook his head. "No, but she wanted to be." He looked at me. "Personally, I'm glad there's another girl around here. Don't tell Bliss that, though."

He winked, a silly gesture that reminded me how green his eyes were and also how nice Noah could be. We had been working together for weeks and I always turned to him with questions about the school or how things were done. Despite talking to him and working with him almost daily, I still didn't know much about him. He was a junior. He was friendly toward everyone, including the freshman boys, who were always coming to him with their incessant questions. He sometimes munched on cinnamon mints, and he usually wore baggy plaid shorts.

Other than those superficial details, I hadn't figured out much about my editing partner. He had a serious interest in video equipment, so he often asked me lots of technical questions, which I was happy to answer. Mr. Morley said we made a good team.

I switched the topic back to the work in front of us. "We need to cut a few minutes from the show. Maybe we can save this footage for another time?"

He nodded. "Sure, but you have to tell Bliss. She's still pissed that we trimmed her segment on the new soda machine."

I rolled my eyes. "Right. What did she say? 'It may not mean much to you, but it matters to hundreds of other students.' She takes herself too seriously."

"We should all take the news seriously," Noah said in a deadpan voice. It was a nearly perfect impersonation of Bliss, and I laughed out loud.

"Really, though, what's her story?" I leaned back in my chair. "She hates me, she bullies the freshmen and she's always dressed like she's about to go on a job interview. I don't get it."

Noah closed the computer program before answering. "She's trying to prove something, I think." He swiveled in his chair to face me. I was always struck by how green his eyes were. I had to stop myself from staring into them.

"She told me once that she's going to be the first person in her family to go to college," Noah continued. "So maybe that's got something to do with her drive. The girl who was the anchor last year gave her a hard time, too, so maybe she's doing the same thing."

"Carrying on a cruel tradition?" I asked. "How noble."

Noah shrugged. "Or maybe she's just a mean and bitter person, I don't know. But I'd like to think there's more to her than that."

"So you're one of those annoying people who believe there's some good in everyone?" I teased.

He smiled. "I'm more like one of those hopeless people who thinks there's something great in everyone."

I swear his eyes sparkled a little when he said it. Not that I was paying attention or anything.

My comfortable routine was interrupted one Wednesday afternoon when the cheerleaders left early for an away game and I was left to take the bus home. I was the last one on and I felt self-conscious as I trudged down the narrow middle aisle, my sandal sticking slightly to something smeared across the floor. I took an empty seat near the back and examined the sole of my shoe, hoping that whatever was now covering my left sole was a food substance and not, as I suspected, some kind of bodily fluid.

"Gross," I muttered, rubbing my shoe against the floor.

"You're just making it worse," a voice behind me said.

I turned, startled. It was Jared, and he was eying my footwear with a kind of half grimace.

"Excuse me?" I was already irritated that I was taking the bus. I wasn't in the mood for criticism.

"You're making it worse," Jared repeated. "It's just going to get dirtier if you rub it on the floor."

"I'm trying to scrape something off," I said.

"Lost cause."

"Thanks for the insight. I'll be sure to consult you the next time I step on something sticky."

Jared chuckled. "Bad day?"

"Something like that." I gave up on the shoe and settled back into my seat, trying not to breathe in too deeply the stench of freshman sweat and plastic seats. The bus was very slowly pulling out of the crowded parking lot.

"You're friends with Avery Macintosh."

"Yes." I didn't turn around. If Jared wanted to keep talking, that was fine, but I didn't intend to keep up a conversation with him.

"But you're not a cheerleader."

"So?" It felt weird to have Jared talking to the back of my head.

"That's interesting."

I gave up and turned around. Jared was sitting back, his arms folded across his chest.

"How is that interesting?"

He shrugged. "Just is."

The bus hit a pothole and everyone bounced a little in their seats. Jared shifted his legs, and I glanced down at them. He noticed.

"Guess you heard all about the crash." He said it softly, but I heard resignation in his voice and felt a twinge of pity. He looked so athletic, so strong. Maybe he'd hoped to earn an athletic scholarship at one point, a future at his top-choice college where he could play football or basketball. I didn't know the extent of his injury, but his pronounced limp told me that any dreams of playing at the college level—at any level, really—had been shattered in the car crash.

"Avery said you were in an accident last year."

Jared sat up straighter. "She said that? She said it was an accident?"

His carefully detached attitude had vanished and he was staring at me intently. I tried to remember the conversation I'd had with Avery. Had she said it was an accident? She had described it that way.

He was driving too fast and he hit a telephone pole.

"I don't know if she actually used the word *accident*," I admitted. "But maybe she did. I think she did."

"You think she did or you know she did? Please, Charlotte. It's important."

It was strange to hear Jared say my name, like he knew me. And he looked so desperate. It *was* important to him.

"She said it was an accident." I was sure of it. Avery certainly didn't say it was intentional. He had been angry at the time, careless.

He's not the same. He's dangerous.

Looking at Jared, I wondered if that was really true. He just didn't strike me as the dangerous type. A loner, maybe. If Avery hadn't been so adamantly against him, I could see myself developing a little crush on him. But I knew from the way my new friends reacted to hearing his name that he was to be avoided. I felt weird even talking to him.

He stared out the window, his eyes wide. "An accident," he mumbled, and I had no idea what had just happened, but I knew I had changed something. And I knew I had to tell Avery.

Jared got off the bus at the first stop without saying anything else to me. I watched from the window as he limped down a tree-lined street. After the bus pulled away, I began to panic. What had I done? Avery would be furious with me if she knew I had talked to him. She would be at the away game late and I didn't know if I'd get a chance to talk to her until the morning.

The bus turned into my neighborhood. I was the only one to get off, and I walked home thinking about things. "I really hate taking the bus," I grumbled. I glanced at our empty driveway and pulled out my house key, knowing my parents were probably off on a local research trip. Before I could put the key into the lock, though, the door swung open.

"Charlotte!"

I jumped a little, then smiled. "Annalise?"

My sister engulfed me in a hug. "It's so good to see you!"

She looked tan and cheerful as she pulled me into the house and we walked into the kitchen together. I paused to kick off my sticky shoes. "What are you doing here?"

She perched on top of one of the bar stools at the kitchen counter while I grabbed something to drink. "I'm here to help you, of course." She set her laptop on the counter and began typing. "I've been doing research," she explained. "I've found some stuff about the Courtyard Café."

I poured myself a soda and sat next to her. "What'd you find?"

"Okay. So, it was built in 1883 as a family residence. But the earthquake in 1886 destroyed the place."

I knew all about the famous earthquake from the carriage tours I'd taken through the city. Charleston had nearly been leveled.

"Who lived there after the earthquake?"

"No one, for a while. It took years to rebuild."

Annalise clicked on a link and brought up a faded photograph showing a group of tents set up outside. It looked like a camp.

A very familiar camp.

"I've seen this before," I murmured.

"I researched the earthquake," Annalise said. "After it happened, people lived in tents made from their tablecloths or curtains for a long time as they rebuilt. They formed little colonies in the nearby parks."

I had seen this exact image in one of my dreams. The dark-haired girl had slipped away from one of these tents in the middle of the night. I was about to tell Annalise all about the dreams when she clicked on a new page and brought up a grainy black-and-white photograph. It was the Courtyard Café, only it was just a house. Two people stood on the porch, but they were blurry.

"Edward and Elizabeth Pickens," Annalise said. "They had one daughter."

"Let me guess. Her name was Charlotte."

"Right. Only, she disappeared after the earthquake."

"You mean she was lost in the rubble?"

"No. She was alive and accounted for. But the day after, she vanished. She was sixteen."

Annalise clicked on some more pages. "Charlotte Pickens disappeared from her family's tent and was never seen again."

"What happened to her?"

Annalise shook her head. "No one knows. Her parents searched for her, but I don't think they ever found her." She typed some more. "I'm trying to locate their graves, but I haven't had any luck yet. They're not listed in any of the cemetery databases. I'll keep trying, though."

I sat there for a while, taking it all in. What had happened to Charlotte Pickens? And why was I seeing her in my dreams?

We needed more information. Her *parents* needed more

information. I was suddenly sure that the two ghostly images I'd seen on the screen, the ones that were now apparently residing in my bedroom, were Edward and Elizabeth Pickens. I was also sure that if we could find out what had happened to their daughter, they would leave me alone. I could feel it.

"So how do we find a girl who's been missing for over a hundred years?" I asked.

Annalise closed her laptop. "I think, dear sister, that you may already know the answer to that."

nine

Again, I was outside at night. The dark-haired girl was walking fast, away from the park and toward the dim streets, her pale dress fluttering around her ankles. She kept her head down as she passed a string of ruined buildings. Chunks of brick and stone had been pushed to the sides of the street, but debris still littered the road and Charlotte was careful to step over the sharp fragments left behind. She came to a side street and turned right, staying close to the broken shells of dark houses.

"Is it you?" someone whispered.

The girl stopped and peered into a gloomy alley. "Yes."

A tall boy emerged from behind a shattered wall. "I could tell by your footsteps."

The girl went to him and they embraced. He had black hair and dark eyes, and his voice was gentle as he put a hand to her belly.

"Are you well?" He spoke with a slight accent, I realized, but I couldn't tell what kind. Spanish? Italian?

She kissed his cheek. "Yes. I am fine."

He led her down the narrow street. "We will head north," he said, helping her step over pieces of rubble. "I have a friend. We can be married tomorrow."

They walked in silence for a while, their arms linked, until they came to a stable. He turned to her. "Are you ready?"

She ran her hand over the mane of one of the waiting horses. "Is one ever ready for such change?"

He cupped her chin in his hand. "It is the only way."

"I know. I will miss them, though."

"We can return one day, when we are established."

The girl closed her eyes. "Promise me I will see them again."

He pulled her into a hug. "I promise you we will come back one day," he whispered into her hair.

"Charlotte?"

I awoke on the dining room sofa. Mom was standing over me.

"Time for school, honey."

I shut my eyes against the sunlight and tried to remember my dream. Something about it felt familiar, yet at the same time so strange. It was like I had been watching a movie clip.

I dragged myself off the sofa, folded my blankets and trudged upstairs to get ready. When I came back downstairs, Mom and Annalise were sitting at the counter, sipping coffee.

"Avery's mom called," Annalise said. "The cheerleaders got a flat tire on the way home last night. Avery's going to be late today, so I'll take you to school."

"Thanks," I mumbled.

The scent of coffee usually helped me wake up, but not today. My eyes felt heavy, my head felt fuzzy, and part of me wanted to sit with Mom and Annalise and tell them every single detail of my dream with the hope that they would dissect it for me, discover its true meaning and insist that I stay home from school to sleep it off. I was about to pull out one of the counter stools when Mom stood up.

"Look at the time. I have a meeting with a woman across town. Possible paranormal activity in an old schoolhouse." She kissed my forehead and left.

"We should get moving, too," Annalise said.

It seemed like only hours earlier my sister had told me I knew how to find Charlotte Pickens, a task that seemed impossible to me.

"How am I supposed to find her when her own parents couldn't?" I had asked, knowing that it wasn't the girl I would actually be searching for, but her grave. She had to have died decades earlier, possibly a full century before I was even born.

Annalise had a theory. She said that the girl's parents didn't think I was their daughter, but for some reason they believed I could locate her resting place.

"You might not know how yet, but there's something about you they connected to, something more than just your name. You're the key, Charlotte. You can find her."

I didn't want to be the key to anything. The ghosts had chosen wrong. They heard their daughter's name spoken aloud and zeroed in on me, and it was all one big supernatural mistake.

"Are you okay?" Annalise asked as we drove to school. "You seem out of it."

I leaned my head back against the seat. "I had a weird dream. It seemed so real. I can't shake it."

"Hmm. Do you think it's connected to what's going on at home?"

"Yes, but I don't know how."

"What exactly do you remember? Don't leave out any details."

I described the girl in the pink dress meeting up with a guy at night and how I thought Charlotte Pickens had run away with him. Certain details played over and over in my head: the boy's voice, thick with a foreign accent; the girl's plea to one day return; the obvious tenderness between the two of them. As I talked, Annalise furrowed her brow.

"Sounds like a scene right after the Charleston earthquake," she said. "We were talking about that yesterday. Maybe your mind was just putting pictures to new information."

It was a logical explanation, but it didn't feel right to me. And as I viewed the images over in my head, something stood out. I remembered Shane telling me that he was going to look over the footage from the Courtyard Café. He wanted to find a connection between the two visits.

Something that's the same.

"The sweater!" I exclaimed. "I wore your pink sweater to the café both times. And the girl in my dreams was wearing pink!"

Annalise glanced at me. "So?"

"The last time her parents saw her, Charlotte Pickens was wearing pink. Your sweater was the trigger. If we just get rid of it, maybe all of this will stop."

We pulled up to the front of the school. Annalise turned off the ignition and looked at me.

"I think we're past the point of getting rid of anything," she said. "Something has started and it's not going to suddenly stop if we throw away a sweater. We have to find the girl."

"No, we don't. Dad says this is merely a stronger kind of energy than we're used to. It's not an intelligent being, Annalise. We don't owe it anything."

"Strong energy? If you really believed that, you wouldn't refer to them as ghosts, which is all I've heard you call them."

"I was only doing that to annoy Mom and Dad."

Annalise raised an eyebrow at me. "Sure. Look, they might chalk all of this up to energy, but I know you. You think it's something more, and I think you're right. So let's do something about it."

I felt a helpless kind of anger build inside of me. Why was my sister pushing this so hard? Just a few months ago she had declared that she wanted nothing to do with paranormal research, yet now she was into it more than I'd ever seen her. What did she expect me to do? I wasn't going to take off on some zany adventure just to locate an old gravestone. The ghosts may have chosen me, but I hadn't chosen them. All I wanted was for things to go back to normal—or as close to normal as I could possibly get.

"Look, if you and Mom and Dad want to put a team together and go off on a ghost hunt, fine. But I'm tired of feeling watched and hearing whispers and dreaming about dead people. Do whatever you want, but leave me out of it."

"We can't leave you out of it."

I glared at her. "Really? Because that's what you've been doing for years."

"That's not true." Her voice was calm and quiet. "We're a team. We've always been a team."

"I am so sick of everyone using that word! We are *not* a team. We are a family. A weird, abnormal family."

"Charlotte, we have to—"

"No! Stop, okay? I don't have to do anything except get to class."

I got out of the car, slammed the door shut and marched into the front doors of the school without looking back. I told myself it wasn't me the ghosts wanted. They weren't even ghosts, I reminded myself. They were balls of energy triggered by the color pink and the sound of my name. It was not my job to do anything about it. My parents had started this, and they could finish it. I was not a paranormal problem solver. I was just a girl trying to get through her senior year without too many complications.

I was twirling the combination on my locker when something sharp poked my shoulder.

"Ow."

"Would you like to explain to me why you cut out my coverage of the Eco Club's tree-planting ceremony?"

I turned to face Bliss Reynolds, who was wearing a pale pink blazer, khaki skirt and sour expression. "Did you just poke me?"

Bliss put her hands on her hips. "That ceremony was important and you had no right to cut it from the morning news. If you think you can sweep in here and sabotage my career—"

"I'm not sabotaging anything! Mr. Morley told me to cut four minutes from the program, which was exactly how long your tree thing was!"

"It wasn't a 'tree thing.' It was an important environmental statement, one that was much more significant than the two-minute segment on Avery and the cheerleaders you chose to keep."

"Bliss, it wasn't my decision, okay? Morley has the final say. You know that." I slammed my locker shut and tried to move past her, but she stepped in front of me.

"No, I don't know that. What I do know is that you have consistently tried to ruin my best work out of some warped loyalty to your friends, and after I meet with the principal this afternoon, your little schemes will be exposed and you, Charlotte Silver, will be dropped from the class."

Bliss flashed a victorious smile. There was something about her self-righteous smirk that set me off. She had made my bad morning even worse, and I was fed up.

"Are you always so paranoid?" I said loudly. People were looking at us, but I didn't care.

"I'm not paranoid. I'm right. You're the one who—"

"Shut up, Bliss! Just shut up! I don't want to hear any more of your insane theories, okay? Just leave me alone!"

Bliss opened her mouth to say something, but nothing came out. Her eyes widened and she put a hand to her throat. For a split second, I thought she was choking.

"Are you okay?" I was aware that a small crowd had formed around us. Everyone was murmuring and looking at Bliss, whose wild eyes and open mouth suggested that something was very wrong. I reached out for her, but she pulled back from me and ran down the hallway. Now everyone was looking at me, waiting for some kind of explanation.

"I don't know what happened," I stammered. "I mean, we were just talking and suddenly she—"

I didn't know how to finish my sentence. Suddenly she what? Lost her ability to speak? Was silenced by my stalker spirits? I pushed past the crowd and raced for the nearest bathroom, where I locked myself inside a stall. I leaned against the wall and tried to pull myself together. What had I done?

The first bell rang, but I stayed where I was. After I was sure the hallways had emptied, I walked to the main office. I decided to fake a migraine and try to get a ride home. I simply couldn't deal with school. Not today.

When I reached the office, I could see a flurry of activity behind the tall windows as two secretaries ushered Bliss into the nurse's office. There was no way I was going in there, so instead I turned around and made my way to the library, where I knew I could find a quiet space between the bookshelves. Sure enough, it was nearly deserted, and the librarian didn't even notice me as I crept into the reference section and slid to the floor.

I didn't know what I was going to do. I couldn't hide between the stacks for the rest of the day, but I couldn't go to the office yet and I couldn't walk home. I would wait a while, I decided. I needed a little time to myself, some quiet to calm my rattled nerves. An hour later, I heard the bell ring for second period. I still wasn't ready to leave my secluded spot, so I stayed put.

"You okay?"

Noah was standing at the end of the aisle. When I shook my head no, he walked closer and squatted down next to me.

"I heard you and Bliss had a little disagreement."

"I'm sure everyone has heard that by now." I sighed. "Only I wouldn't call it little."

"It'll blow over. She's harmless. Intense, but harmless."

"Yeah, well, apparently I'm not."

Noah gave me a funny look. "What do you mean?"

"Nothing. Is Bliss still in the nurse's office? Is she okay?" What I really wanted to know was if she could talk, but I knew that question would seem totally insane.

"She's fine. I just saw her in the hallway on her way to class."

"Did she say anything?"

He chuckled. "She told me to do a better job at editing her footage."

I felt an immediate sense of relief. I hadn't permanently injured Bliss. I'd caused something to happen, but it had passed and maybe everything would be fine.

Noah switched from squatting to sitting. "Does your, uh, problem with Bliss have anything to do with that article she wrote last year?"

"What article? I wasn't even here last year."

"Yeah, I know, but I thought, since you're friends with Avery, that maybe she told you about it."

So many things seemed to come back to my friendship with Avery. It had somehow become one of my defining characteristics. Jared had mentioned it on the bus, Bliss had brought it up during our fight, and now Noah. It was weird being identified first and foremost as Avery's friend. Nothing else seemed quite as important to other people.

"Avery told me that Bliss had written a negative article about the cheerleaders," I told Noah. "But she didn't elaborate."

"The cheerleaders?" Noah looked confused. "I must have missed that one. No, I'm talking about the big article, the one about the accident."

Now it was my turn to be confused. "Jared's accident?"

"Well, yeah, but it was more than that."

"How do you mean?"

Noah stared at me for a moment. "I think you need to read it. I'll go through the archives and find you a copy." He glanced around. "I need to get back to class. I'm supposed to be returning a book for my science teacher. Will you be in AV later?"

"I think I'm going to go home early today."

Noah stood up. "Okay, then. I'll see you tomorrow. Take it easy, Charlotte."

After the next bell rang, I went to the office complaining of an imaginary migraine. I called home but no one answered, so I spent the next few class periods lying on a cot in the nurse's room, where I fell asleep for a while. Thankfully, I didn't have another weird dream.

When I woke up I forgot for a second where I was. I could hear a phone ringing and the tapping of a keyboard. The nurse came in.

"Oh, good. You're awake. How are you feeling?"

"Better. What time is it?"

She looked at her watch. "Almost time for the final bell. Do you have a ride home?"

I hadn't seen Avery or Callie or any of the other girls all day, but I was sure they had returned from their unexpectedly extended away game.

"Yeah, I've got a ride," I said. "Thanks."

I walked through the empty hallways to my locker. I knew I would have a ton of homework to catch up on and hoped Callie or one of the other cheerleaders would have the assignments, so I crammed nearly every book from my locker into my backpack and lugged it to the doors. The bell rang and people swarmed into the hallways. I stood against a wall, waiting to catch a glimpse of Avery. Minutes passed and I worried that I had missed her or worse, that she thought I hadn't come to school at all. I headed for the parking lot and ran into Callie.

"You're here!" she said. "We missed you at lunch."

"I was in the nurse's office with a headache. I heard you guys had a crazy night."

We walked toward the senior lot together. "The bus got a

flat," Callie explained. "We made it home after three in the morning, so the principal gave us all a late pass, but we had to show up before noon."

"You should have gotten the day off."

Callie laughed. "That's what I said! But we had to be here to set an example or something. The school can't let people think that we get special treatment or—"

She stopped, a strange expression on her face. I looked in the direction she was staring and saw Avery standing next to her car. A guy was in front of her, his back to us. I couldn't hear what they were saying, but Avery looked visibly upset. As Callie and I got closer, Avery covered her face with both hands and sobbed.

"Get away from her!" Callie yelled, breaking into a sprint.

The guy turned around. It was Jared. "I just wanted to talk to her," he said, taking a step back. I was aware of people pointing and staring. Callie opened the driver's side door for Avery and practically pushed her inside. Jared just stood there, watching.

"I need to talk to her," he said. "Five minutes. That's all. I just need five minutes."

"Get in," Callie said to me. I nodded and slid into the passenger seat.

Callie turned to Jared. "You are not to come near her, do you understand?" She pointed a finger at his chest. "Do not even look at her. Ever."

Callie tapped on my window and I rolled it down.

"Make sure she gets home okay," she said to me. "Avery? I'm coming over to your house. I'll be right behind you." She jogged off toward her car.

Avery was crying softly. "Do you want me to drive?" I asked.

She shook her head. "I'll be fine," she mumbled. She took a deep breath. "Sorry I'm such a mess."

"Don't worry about it. Seriously. I just want you to be okay." I found a clean tissue in my purse and handed it to her.

Avery took the tissue and wiped at her eyes. She looked up. Through the window we could see Jared as he limped back toward the school. People parted for him, backing away as if he were contaminated.

"What did he do?" I asked, remembering that I had meant to tell her about my conversation the day before with Jared.

I wasn't sure that she even heard me. She just kept looking intently out the window like she was making sure he was really leaving. A few seconds later, she responded, her voice cold and hard.

"He killed my boyfriend."

ten

"I just couldn't tell you," Avery said. We were in her room, sitting on the floor surrounded by crumpled tissues. Her eyes gleamed red, but she was done crying. The other girls had left after spending an hour reassuring her that they would not allow Jared to come near her ever again.

Before they left, Callie pulled me aside. "Can you stay until her mom gets home from work?"

"Of course." I needed to stay. I needed to hear the whole story straight from Avery, and after everyone left, that's what she did—explained everything, every secret she'd kept from me—until I understood.

The clock on the dresser ticked and the room filled with a golden glow from the setting sun. I reflected on everything Avery had told me about Adam since we met. *He was a senior last year,* she had said. *He got into Michigan.* She never said that's where he was now, only that he'd gotten into college. *I talk to him every day, but still. It's hard.* I had assumed they called each other. She probably did talk to him every day, I thought. He just wasn't able to respond.

"Ever since it happened, everyone has treated me like a victim," Avery said as we sat in her room. "It made people so uncomfortable that most of them just stopped talking to me, but I could see it in their faces—they pitied me." She took a deep breath. "I thought finally, here was someone who didn't know, someone who wouldn't treat me like a walking tragedy."

I told her I understood, and I did, in a way. I'd never been pitied, but once people knew what my parents did for a living, they began to change. At first they would think my odd distinction was great and I was inevitably invited to Halloween parties, where everyone would stand around watching me like I could conjure dead people into the room. When the initial cool factor wore out, the rumors started, usually stuff about late-night séances that supposedly went on at home or how my parents were actually hunting vampires or were storing withered corpses in the basement. The weirder, the better—people seemed to believe only the craziest rumors, and instead of invitations to parties I received strange looks and cold shoulders.

"Tell me about that night," I said. "What happened?"

Avery looked over at her dresser, where the framed photos of Adam stood arranged in a half circle. "We went to a party to celebrate the first day of spring break," she began. "Only, I didn't want to go. Dante had run off. He was missing and I wanted to stay home in case he came back."

The tiny dog heard his name and poked his head through the doorway. Avery patted the carpet and he trotted over and curled up next to her, but not before stopping to growl at me first.

"Adam insisted. He said it would do me some good to get out and stop worrying for a while." She paused to rub Dante's belly.

"It was just your typical party," Avery went on. "Loud. Crowded. Normally, I would have loved it. But I was worried about Dante, and Adam was hanging out with his friends more than me.

"I told him I needed to go home and asked if I could borrow his car. We didn't have a fight or anything, but we didn't kiss goodbye, either. He said he'd call me the next day, and I left. It was the last time I saw him alive."

Avery was slowly petting Dante, and soon his beady little eyes closed.

"His mom called late that night. She said there'd been an accident. She said it was bad. Very, very bad." She kept her eyes focused on her dog, who was now asleep. "Her voice sounded so broken, so hollow. And I knew. I knew that Adam was dead."

"How does Jared fit in to all of this?" I asked.

Avery winced at the sound of his name. "He arrived at the party after I left. Callie overheard them talking. She said Jared was upset about something and said he needed to talk to Adam alone. They left together, in Jared's car.

"They were on Main Street. A witness saw the car jerk suddenly to the left, then it crashed into a telephone pole."

She looked at me. "It wasn't an accident. Jared intentionally hit that pole."

I frowned. "Why do you think that?"

"I went to see him at the hospital. He told me about the fight. He admitted that he had been driving and that the accident was his fault." She looked down at her hands. "Jared had a death wish. Problem is, the wrong person died."

"I'm really sorry," I said. "What can I do?"

"I'm the one who's sorry. I should have told you, Charlotte."

"It's okay. I understand why you didn't."

Avery nodded. "Just don't treat me any differently, okay? No sympathy, no pity. Promise."

"I promise."

My cell phone rang and I reached into my backpack. "It's my mom. I forgot to tell her where I was going after school." I flipped open the phone.

"Charlotte, thank God! Where are you? The school called and said you missed classes today!"

"I'm fine, Mom. I'm at Avery's. I'll be home soon."

"Did something happen? What's going on?"

"I'll explain later. Everything's fine. Really."

How was I going to explain my day to her? Everything was not fine. I got into a fight with my sister, my phantom followers had attacked Bliss and my new best friend had come undone in front of my eyes. Avery was trying to pretend that she was handling her boyfriend's death, but her anguish was still there, waiting to be triggered. I understood now why she always steered clear of Main Street and why she was such a careful driver. She was building a life around avoidance, trying to keep away from anything that might bring back painful memories.

I got off the phone and told Avery that I needed to head home soon. "You going to be okay?"

Avery gave me a sad smile. "Sure. Time heals all wounds, right?"

"I don't think so."

She looked surprised. I continued, "Time teaches you how

to live with your wounds. It doesn't erase them. Not completely."

Avery hugged me. "Thank you. You're the first person who hasn't said that I'll forget all of this one day."

"You won't. But it'll get better, I know it."

I walked home hoping that what I had said was true. I didn't have a lot of personal experience with grief, but in my parents' line of work, I'd been around it and had witnessed how people dealt with losing someone. There were those who spent the rest of their lives mourning and those who went on living. I truly hoped that Avery would be in the second group, but she wasn't there yet. Of course, I reminded myself, Adam's death had occurred less than a year before. No one could expect her to bounce right back. She needed time and support.

And eventually, she needed to face Jared.

There was still so much Avery didn't know. What had happened in the car that night? Why had Jared swerved directly into the telephone pole? I had spoken to him only twice, but he didn't strike me as having a death wish, like Avery had said. Only Jared had the answers. I remembered the newspaper article Noah talked about. What had Bliss written that had angered Avery so much? I hoped Noah would find me a copy soon.

My parents were waiting for me as soon as I walked in the front door. I'd never caused the school to call home before, and they seemed confused as to whether they should be really angry or really worried. Shane was in the living room, so they didn't yell too much. I kept telling them that everything was fine, but they weren't buying it, so I came clean about what happened with Bliss.

"What do you mean, she lost her voice?" Dad asked.

"It was like she couldn't talk. She was fine later. But it was scary."

Shane called us over to the living room. He had the Courtyard Café footage displayed on his monitor. "I think Charlotte's right about the trigger being the color pink," he said. "But there's more to it. Watch this."

I watched the footage of me and Annalise, but nothing new stood out. When the clip ended Shane turned to us. "Did you catch it?"

Mom frowned. "No. What are we looking for?"

"Three things happen immediately before the white figures appear. Watch the second clip."

After the second clip, I understood. "It's the color pink, my name and the sound of my voice. Those three things combined form the trigger?"

Shane clapped his hands together. "Exactly!"

I sat down next to him. "Great. So I'll ask people to call me Charlie instead of Charlotte. Problem solved."

"Not quite." Shane swiveled in his chair to face my parents. "There's energy when even one of the triggers is present. It's only when all three happen at the same time that the energy manifests itself." He looked at me. "So unless you change your name, stop talking and are never around anything pink, the energy will remain in some form, even if it's weakened."

"Okay, plan B. We throw some holy water around, say a couple of prayers and send these guys back to Charleston."

Mom sighed. "Charlotte, I wish it were that simple. Once energy like this is triggered, it's unlikely to just stop."

Dad adopted his professional voice. "Think of it this way—a boulder is rolling down a hill. That boulder will stay in motion and keep rolling until it hits something bigger than itself, something strong enough to bring it to a standstill. I'm afraid we need something stronger than removing one trigger to stop this kind of energy."

"What about what I need? I need this thing, whatever it is, to leave me alone!" I could feel tears burning in my eyes. I didn't want to hear about big boulders. My parents were the paranormal experts. Why couldn't they take care of this without me? It shouldn't be up to teenaged girls to usher restless sprits into the afterlife. I had enough problems of my own without the dilemmas of dead people added to the list.

Mom rubbed my shoulder. "We'll figure this out, honey. We'll help you."

I realized someone was missing from our little gathering. "Where's Annalise?"

Mom stopped rubbing. "She left this afternoon."

"Left for where?"

Dad was putting on headphones. "She went back to school."

"Oh." I couldn't believe that Annalise had left without saying goodbye to me. She'd never done that before. Of course, we'd never really fought like that, with me storming off and her driving away. "When is she coming back?"

Mom was looking over my shoulders at the monitors. "We'll see her at Thanksgiving," she mumbled. Thanksgiving was nearly two months away. I needed to speak to Annalise before then. I couldn't bear to have my sister angry with me for that long. I reasoned that I should give her a little time to cool off, though. A few days, maybe.

Mom was distracted, so I slipped out of my chair and went upstairs.

I had been staying away from my room over the past few weeks, sleeping downstairs and grabbing clean clothes directly from the laundry room. I stood in my bedroom doorway for a moment, feeling like a stranger. I crossed the room and sat on my still-made bed.

"I don't know how to help you," I said out loud. I kept my voice low, almost a whisper. It felt silly to be talking to myself. Annalise had been right, though—I did think we were dealing with something that was more than just energy. I really felt that whatever it was possessed some sort of intelligence, although I couldn't explain why.

"Can you hear me? It's Charlotte. I don't know what I'm supposed to do for you."

I waited for some kind of acknowledgment. A sound or a feeling. Anything. After a few minutes, I got up and searched for something pink. I found Annalise's sweater balled up on the floor and grabbed it, then sat back down on my bed.

"Okay, one more time. This is Charlotte. I know you're here."

I thought I saw a shadow out of the corner of my eye. I took a deep breath.

"Right. So you can hear me. I know you're looking for your daughter, but I don't know how to find her. I need help."

I wished I had brought the EVP recorder upstairs. Maybe they were talking to me but I couldn't hear them. I was about to go downstairs when it happened.

Someone sat down next to me.

I felt the pressure on the mattress, and when I looked over, there was an indentation on my bedspread. I slowly moved my hand over the spot. It felt icy cold. I pulled my hand back. The hair on the back of my neck prickled.

Someone was sitting next to me.

Someone I couldn't see or hear, but I *felt* them, as surely as I would have felt my mom or dad if they had sat down. I stiffened and wished that I hadn't triggered them while I was alone. They were getting stronger, strong enough that I could feel them, and it terrified me.

"I can't do this," I whispered. "I can't find her for you."

Whatever had been sitting next to me immediately got up. I panicked. Had I made it angry?

"I'm sorry, really I am, but I just can't. I don't know how."

I stood up to leave, but at that moment I heard a scratching sound coming from my nightstand. I froze. I didn't want to turn around and look. Something was happening directly behind me and I did not want to look at it. I could feel my heart pounding, could feel my legs glued in place. My bedroom door was open, but I was convinced that if I tried to run, it would slam shut in my face and I would be trapped. I opened my mouth.

"Mom!" I screamed as loud as I could. "Dad!"

They heard the fear in my voice and began running up the stairs. Shane was shouting something about grabbing a camera. My parents burst into my room. Dad was looking everywhere, trying to figure out what was going on, but Mom came over to me right away.

"What happened? Are you okay?"

"Something was in here with me. I heard scratching. On the nightstand."

Dad walked over to the little table and looked at it. "Karen, you should see this."

Mom got up. "Oh, my."

I still couldn't bring myself to look. "What is it?"

"A message. It looks like it was scratched into the wood."

Dad crouched on the ground and plucked something from the floor. "A picture hook," he said, holding it up. I saw a small hole in the wall where the hook had been.

"What does the message say?" I asked, my voice wobbly.

When they didn't answer me right away, I turned around and inched closer to the nightstand. There, in scraggly letters, read just two words.

You will.

eleven

Noah gave me the newspaper article about Adam and Jared's accident the very next day during AV class.

"Don't let anyone else see it," he whispered as he slipped me the folded page. "They might, you know, freak out a little."

I nodded and slid the paper into my backpack. "No problem. I'll read it at home."

I'd had enough of people freaking out. The school was buzzing with rumors about Jared and Avery's confrontation in the parking lot the day before. Thankfully, Jared didn't show up for school, but the cheerleaders were on high alert. If they overheard someone talking about what had happened, they confronted that person or stared them down. They were a force to be reckoned with, particularly when Avery was involved.

It was strange, but I finally felt like I fit in with the other girls. I now knew the big secret-that-wasn't-really-a-secret, and I shared the other girls' commitment to keeping Avery safe from vicious gossip. I also felt more bonded with Avery.

We shared a common goal, even though she didn't know it: we both wanted to be treated as totally normal. Of course, Avery *was* normal, but dealing with tragedy, whereas I was dealing with ghosts who were getting stronger every day and taking a more active role in my life.

You will. The two words etched into my nightstand felt tattooed on my brain. You will what? You will help us, no matter how hard you fight it? Or you will know *how* to help us? I couldn't decide whether it was a threat or a prediction.

Or both.

"Charlotte, you there?"

I blinked. Noah was watching me.

"Sorry. I was daydreaming."

"Right." He motioned to the computer screen. "I asked if you thought we should lead with the tree ceremony or the soccer highlights."

My answer was automatic. "Tree ceremony."

I hadn't seen Bliss since our strange confrontation. She was avoiding me, and I was fine with that. I was making a more conscious effort to balance the sports footage with other news, and the tree ceremony was my attempt at apologizing. Bliss had been out of line, but rendering her speechless in the hallway was something I felt guilty about.

I tried to focus on editing, but my mind kept wandering back to my paranormal problem. The main question I had to answer was what had happened to Charlotte Pickens. If I could figure that out, maybe I could find her final resting place and lead her parents there.

I nudged Noah. "I have a question for you."

He frowned at the screen. "Is it why Bliss is wearing purple and green? Because she shouldn't. She kind of looks like an eggplant."

I laughed. "No comment. But seriously, can I ask you something?"

He turned his chair toward me. "Ask away."

"Have you ever known someone who ran away from home?"

He raised an eyebrow at me. "Do I need to be worried?"

"No, it's not me. Promise. It's for this, uh, documentary my parents are working on."

"Well, if it's for the advancement of documentary film, then yes, I do know someone who ran away from home. My mom."

"You're kidding."

"Nope. She left home at seventeen."

"Wow." I hesitated before asking my next question, unsure if I was getting too personal. "Can I ask why?"

"She and my dad kind of...eloped."

"How romantic!"

Noah blushed. He was cute when he did that, I thought. If he was only another year older, he'd be perfect boyfriend material. Now I was blushing, I was sure of it. I doubted that Noah saw me that way. We worked well together and had interesting conversations, but he'd never even hinted that he saw me as anything other than a friend, and I was okay with that. Callie had been talking a lot lately about wanting to set me up with Harris Abbott, a senior on the football team. I wasn't sure I was ready to add a boyfriend to the chaos that was my life, and I definitely didn't want to go on a blind date, but the concept of lumbering through my entire senior year without being kissed was more than a little depressing.

Noah pulled me out of my thoughts. "I wouldn't call my parents' situation romantic." He ran a hand through his hair. "My mom was pregnant with my older brother and my grandparents didn't approve of my dad."

"Oh."

"It worked for a while, I guess. But it was hard. Mom was married with three kids before she turned twenty-one. And my dad split when I was four."

"I'm sorry."

Noah shrugged. "It is what it is. Anyway, I hope that helps with your parents' film."

"It does, actually. Thanks."

Noah's scenario made sense. If Charlotte Pickens was in love and her parents didn't approve, that may have been reason to leave. In my dream, the girl had seemed sad to go. She whispered goodbye and turned back to look at her family's tent one last time. She knew she might not ever come back. Was it possible that she was pregnant, as well? It would have been a solid reason for a girl in the 1800s to vanish. Maybe she wanted to spare her parents certain public humiliation.

I needed Annalise to conduct more research for me. If we could find the name of a boy who also went missing around the time of the earthquake, we might have something to go on.

After I got home from school, I pulled out the article Noah had found for me. It was dated from the previous March. "Senior Class Mourns One of Its Own," read the title. Bliss Reynolds was listed as the writer.

While Spring Break is usually a time for celebration, this year it will be remembered as a time of mourning after a late-night accident claimed the life of Lincoln High senior Adam Roth. Roth was a passenger in a car driven by Jared James, a junior. James remains in critical condition at Mercy South Hospital.

Both Roth and James attended a party earlier in the evening. They left together just after midnight and were traveling south down Main Street when James lost control of the car and struck a telephone pole. Roth was pronounced dead at the scene. James suffered head trauma and several broken bones. His mother, Evelyn James, said that it is unlikely her son will recover completely.

"Please pray for my son," she said.

Witnesses said that a moment before striking the telephone pole, James's car swerved sharply. Police have ruled out alcohol as a factor in the crash, but do not know why James lost control of the vehicle.

"The accident remains under investigation," said Officer Lettrick, who was first at the scene. James was conscious only briefly and told his mother that Roth grabbed the steering wheel, causing the car to crash.

Roth, 18, had recently been accepted to the University of Michigan on a full football scholarship. Teammate Harris Abbott said he will remember Roth as a strong athlete, loyal friend and "an all-around great guy."

"We have lost a wonderful young man who was full of tremendous potential," Coach Roberts said. "Adam will be sorely missed and fondly remembered."

The funeral service was held last week. A memorial service for the entire school will be held tomorrow afternoon in the gymnasium.

I read through the article twice, but only one thing stood out to me. Had Adam really grabbed the wheel, causing the car to crash? Or was Jared simply trying to avoid blame? It wasn't as scandalous as I had thought it would be. Avery's anger had to stem from the suggestion that the accident was Adam's fault. The article did confirm one thing for me, though—there was more to the story than Avery was saying.

My parents had been dividing their time between examining the footage taken at home and filming at nearby historical sites. They weren't having much luck with either project, though. Most of the local "hauntings" were easily debunked, and we needed more facts before we could move forward in the search for Charlotte Pickens. When they got home later that evening, I shared my theory about what may have caused her to run away.

"Annalise has access to a lot of historical records in Charleston," Mom said. "She'll keep us posted."

I knew I should call my sister, but I wasn't ready to have her yell at me. Instead, I decided to wait awhile so I could plan out the perfect apology.

The next week went by smoothly. Jared didn't return to school, and there were rumors that he had dropped out for good. Thankfully, people turned their attention to Homecoming. I helped the cheerleaders decorate paper masks, which we then plastered throughout the hallways. I liked the idea of a masquerade theme. I would be able to dress up, don a mask and blend in with the crowd.

I fell back into my comfortable routine of going to class, eating lunch with the cheerleaders and editing footage with Noah, who I was starting to look forward to seeing every day. I liked that he was serious about his work and had goals to study film production in college.

"What about you?" he asked. It was a Friday afternoon. We were sitting in front of the monitor where we always worked while Mr. Morley explained splicing scenes to a small group of freshmen at the front of the room.

"What about me?" I asked.

"You're a senior. Do you know where you'll be going to college next year?"

"Charleston, probably."

The truth was, I hadn't given college the same amount of

thought and consideration as the other seniors had. I would see them before class, poring over the glossy catalogs or discussing application essays. I had applied to Charleston before we moved simply because that's where Annalise was, and I was afraid that if I went somewhere out of state we would never see each other. My parents didn't have a home base, they were always traveling, and I didn't want to spend Christmas in a hotel room while my parents visited. If both Annalise and I were going to the same school, our parents could come to us, and at least we'd all be together a few times each year.

Still, part of me wanted to attend school somewhere else. I wasn't sure where, exactly, but I'd looked up schools online and had sent away for applications, just so I could have some options. It was the last week of September, and I knew I was running out of time.

College was still on my mind when I got home that afternoon, and I was pleased to find several school information packets crammed into the mailbox. As I pulled them out, though, another piece of mail caught my eye, and I groaned.

"Oh, no."

I grabbed everything and rushed inside, spilling the bills and catalogs across the kitchen counter. None of it mattered except the one thing, the one awful thing, that I held in my hands.

My time was up.

By Monday, it would be over.

twelve

My parents weren't smiling. Instead, they looked at me with serious expressions, the ones they used when they were investigating something unusual. Behind them floated Annalise, shrouded in a neon-green haze.

At the end of each month we received a channel guide. It was a bulky magazine that featured hundreds of pages of TV schedules, as well as a dozen pages dedicated to that month's "Best Bets." Everyone in town got a copy unless they owned a satellite dish. Usually we just recycled them, but I knew this issue would be different. My parents would add this one to their collection of memorabilia.

They were on the cover.

"October's Best Bet: A Silver Spirits Marathon," screamed the title. I flipped to the article, a four-page layout that included more pictures and a column of "Fun Facts" about my family:

- Patrick and Karen Silver have been married for 23 years,

but have been researching the supernatural together for over 25 years!
- They have two daughters: Annalise, 20, and Charlotte, 17.
- The first "Silver Spirits" documentary aired on the day Annalise was born.
- The Silvers have produced 60 one-hour documentaries and have published four books together.
- The Silver family presently resides in South Carolina.

I sighed. Although I wasn't in any of the pictures—it was mainly my parents and a few with Shane—I had been mentioned by name. And the marathon would run all month, with two episodes airing each night. I could be seen in a few of those, often in the background but sometimes in the closing credits, too.

"This is not good," I muttered.

"This is great!" Mom exclaimed from behind me. I jumped. "Didn't mean to startle you," she said, picking up the magazine. "Did this arrive today?"

"Yeah."

"Your dad will be thrilled. We'll add it to the collection."

The collection consisted of every newspaper or magazine they'd ever been mentioned in, all stored by date in twenty brightly colored plastic storage bins. When we moved to our new house, I worried that my parents might hang some of the framed covers in our new house, but they didn't want to put nails in the walls.

"We're moving in a year," Dad had said. "Let's try to keep the place looking new."

I was relieved. There was no way I could bring people over if the walls displayed a gallery of memorabilia dedicated to my parents' bizarre career. The bins had been safely stacked in the garage to gather cobwebs.

"I'm not happy about this," I told Mom. I followed her from the kitchen to the dining room. She moved my pillow aside on the sofa and sat down to read the article.

"Not happy about what?"

"The channel guide. Now everyone will know that we're freaks."

"Charlotte, stop. We are not freaks."

I flopped down next to Mom. "Well, we're not normal. And after the school sees this, I'll be crowned Queen of the Weird."

She smiled. "The Princess of the Paranormal."

It was an old joke. The dedication page of their third book had read, "To Charlotte, our paranormal princess." I was five and had been going around telling everyone I wanted to be a princess when I grew up. At first, the dedication had thrilled me, but then other kids began to tease me about it. It had been a long time ago, but every once in a while someone I'd never met before would comment on it.

"This is serious, Mom. You have no idea how crazy it can get."

She closed the magazine and looked at me. "Yes, I do. And I also know how crazy *you* can get when you think everyone's talking about you. Believe me, Charlotte, most people are more concerned with themselves than what someone else's parents do for a living. Besides, your friends don't care."

"That's because my friends don't know."

"We've lived here for over two months and you haven't told anyone?"

I shook my head. "No."

Mom sighed. "Well, it needs to come from you. Otherwise, they'll think you really *are* hiding something strange."

I started to say that I *was*, but Mom held up her hand. "Don't say it. Honey, I love you, but I'm worried. You tend to avoid your problems rather than face them. Maybe it's time to change that."

She got up and left the room, leaving me to fume over her words. I didn't avoid my problems. I just didn't feel as though I had to focus on them every minute of every day. And telling people about certain aspects of my life would only create trouble. If I was guilty of anything, it was of trying not to bring new problems into my life. That wasn't avoidance. That was logical thinking.

After a while I realized there was only one person I could talk to, only one who would understand exactly what I was going through. I picked up the phone and dialed her number.

"Hello?"

"Annalise? It's me."

"Hey." She was quiet, so I figured she was still mad at me.

"Look, I'm really sorry for yelling at you and storming off like that. I was upset, but I shouldn't have taken it out on you."

"No, you shouldn't have. But I get it. You've had a lot to deal with lately."

"You have no idea."

I described for Annalise everything that had happened since she had returned to school, starting with my strange encounter with Bliss. I told her about Avery's secret, the etching in my nightstand and my theory that Charlotte Pickens had run away from home because she was pregnant. Finally, I explained the channel guide and how my own secret was now exposed.

"You know how it is," I said. "The last time everyone found out, it was a disaster. It took about two weeks before half the school was convinced I belonged to some kind of cult. Eva Landon told me she prayed for my soul every morning."

"How did you deal with it?" Annalise asked.

"We moved after Thanksgiving, so I didn't have to."

"Well, at least you didn't avoid the problem."

"Very funny. It wasn't my fault that we moved."

"No, but Mom has a point. You don't like to deal with stuff." I could hear Annalise moving things around on her desk. "I mean, you don't face your problems head-on. You just try to leave them behind you. Problem is, this time you're stuck. Mom and Dad aren't moving again until the summer."

"Thanks for the psychological evaluation," I muttered.

"Charlotte, I'm trying to help. Don't be defensive."

"Fine. Help me. What do I do now?"

"Like I said, it's time to confront your problems. That means talking to Bliss, coming clean with Avery and dealing with your ghosts. No more evasion."

I knew she was right, but none of it was going to be easy. There was so much to lose. What if Bliss made me angry and something else happened? It would be my fault. What if Avery and Callie and the other girls freaked out on me? I'd have to find new friends all over again. What if the ghosts got stronger and I failed at finding their daughter? I'd be stuck with powerful, persistent spirits following my every move.

"Have you found anything new on the Pickenses?" I asked.

Annalise sighed. "No, which is pretty odd, actually. They owned property in Charleston, and the house was in their

name for a long time, but I can't find their death certificates or anything. They must have moved, but I have no idea
where."

"Great. So now we're searching for three graves, not just
one."

Annalise promised to keep researching in Charleston, and
I promised to do more to manage my situation at home. After
we hung up, I wandered into the kitchen, where Shane was
making a sandwich at the counter. He was wearing a faded
black concert T-shirt and a pair of headphones around his
neck.

"Hey, kid, how you doing?"

"Fine." I pulled a pitcher of iced tea from the fridge and
poured myself a glass. "I talked with Annalise." I sipped my
drink.

Shane sat down. "Did you? Good. I heard you had a little
disagreement before she left."

"I apologized. We're good now."

"Glad to hear it." Shane watched me drink my tea, and I
thought about how he was like an uncle to me. He'd taught
me how to ride a bike and hold a video camera and make omelets. When I was little I worried that he'd meet a woman, get
married and leave us behind. Now I worried that he wouldn't
get married and would be single and lonely for the rest of his
life.

"This must be rough for you," he said. "I mean, I've seen
some freaky stuff over the years, but this one beats all."

I set down my glass. "Yeah."

"I've never seen your folks so worried." He lowered his
voice. "Your mom's been talking to psychics. Don't tell her I
told you that, though."

I almost choked on my tea. "Psychics? Mom doesn't believe in psychics!"

Shane laughed. "I know. But she figures there might be someone who could help. Once we find this girl, we have to do something to give her parents closure, you know? Your mom thinks there might be some kind of ceremony or prayer or something we'll need."

I hadn't thought that far ahead. If we did locate the final resting place of Charlotte Pickens, what then? I guess I had assumed that her parents would be following me around. They would see the tombstone and that would be that. But something about that scenario felt incomplete, in a way. It couldn't be so simple.

I pointed to Shane's headphones. "What are you working on today?"

"The Charleston footage. We're trying to scrape enough together for a one-hour special."

"I thought you'd be using the stuff from the Courtyard Café. There's more than enough tape."

Shane shook his head. "Nah. We don't want to use what's happening to you. That's family business."

I was surprised. All this time, I figured my parents were interested in figuring out what was going on so they could produce another TV episode.

"By the way, I've rigged your room with everything we've got. Thermal camera, digital recorders—the works. If something happens, we'll get it on tape."

Shane returned to his work and I went back to the dining room. If everyone else was confronting my problems, it was time for me to do the same.

I picked up the phone and called Avery.

"Can you come over?" I asked. "I need to talk to you about something."

"I'm on my way out the door, actually. My mom's having car trouble. I need to pick her up at work."

I glanced at the clock. It was nearly six. "Can you come over after that?"

"Sure. I should be back in less than an hour. Is everything all right?"

"Yes. I just—well, I need to tell you in person."

"Got it. I'll be over later."

I felt better after I hung up the phone. Nervous, but glad that I was going to come clean with Avery. No more secrets, no more avoiding things.

I turned on the TV and flipped through the channels, hoping to find some mindless entertainment so I wouldn't have to think about what I was going to say to Avery. I had just settled on a game show when the doorbell rang.

"I'll get it!" I called to Shane. Maybe Avery hadn't gone to pick up her mom after all, I thought. Time to face the music. I took a deep breath and opened the door.

It wasn't Avery standing on my front porch.

It was Jared.

"What are you—"

"I need your help," he interrupted. His face was red and he was out of breath as though he'd run the entire way to my house, which I knew wasn't possible.

"What are you talking about?"

Jared took an awkward step forward. "Please, Charlotte. Help me. I'm desperate."

thirteen

Jared stepped into the foyer before I could stop him.

"You can't be here," I said. "Avery's coming over soon and she'll go ballistic if she sees you."

"I won't stay long. Ten minutes." He reached for my arm. "Please. I need to talk to you."

I looked past him. Outside, the street was empty, but Avery could drive by at any moment. I closed the front door.

"Ten minutes. Then you have to leave."

He nodded. "I need to sit down. I walked here."

I knew from where the school bus had dropped him off that he lived at least two miles away. With his limp, it should have taken Jared a long time to get to my house. I led him to the dining room, where he collapsed onto the sofa.

"I don't understand why you're here," I said.

He was still trying to catch his breath. I felt bad for him, so I went to the kitchen and got him a glass of water. He drank it in one long gulp.

"Thanks," he said when he was finished. I stood across from

him and waited with my arms crossed over my chest. Finally, he spoke.

"I didn't kill Adam."

"I never said you did."

He looked at me. "A lot of people believe I did."

"Why is that?" I asked. It didn't make sense to me. Even after listening to Avery's version of events, I couldn't figure out why the entire school hated Jared. Even if the accident had been his fault, he had obviously suffered. No one seemed to have any pity for him, though.

"They think that I killed Adam because that's what I told them."

I sat down. "Okay, you're going to have to make a little more sense. Why did you tell them that?"

He leaned his head back on the sofa and closed his eyes. "I had to. Avery wouldn't let it go. She kept coming to see me at the hospital, asking questions."

"And you said you killed your best friend?"

"It was my fault. I was to blame."

I was having trouble processing everything. "You just said you didn't kill Adam. Now you're saying that you're to blame. Help me out here, Jared."

Jared opened his eyes. "Adam is dead because of me, but it was an accident. After it happened, though, I told Avery a different story."

"Why?"

His voice was quiet. "I can't tell you."

"Can't tell me or won't tell me?"

"I can't. I promised Adam I wouldn't. And now I need his permission to tell everyone the truth."

"What?" I was shocked. "Jared, you're going to have to explain—"

"No." He sat up straight. "Look, I saw the channel guide article and I know who you are. I have to contact Adam, and you can help me. It's the only way to prove that I didn't kill my best friend. It's the only way I can move on, and the only way I know to help Avery do the same."

"Whoa. I don't know what you think I can do, but let me tell you right now I can't talk to dead people. It's not like that."

Jared stood up. "I've seen the show. I know you can do it."

"It's not like we have a spirit phone," I protested. "We don't just call the other side and ask to speak to a specific person."

"Adam died too soon. He's still here. I feel him. We'll just go back to the scene of the accident—"

"No! Jared, I promise you, he's not there."

One of the biggest misconceptions people had was that ghosts hung around the place they died. But in my parents' experience, that was true only if the person died in the place they had lived. Their energy lingered in the area that held the most emotional connection for the person during their lifetime.

My parents had another theory, too, one that tried to explain why some energy lingered for years. They found that the locations with the most activity tended to be places where people had spent a great deal of time before they died. For example, old prisons or asylums were usually incredibly active, almost crowded with energy. Mom and Dad believed that some people made a conscious choice to leave energy behind, usually because they had some unfinished business that they felt passionate about. Their intense emotions lingered until something triggered the leftover energy, releasing it. My parents weren't sure how this happened, but it was something they studied intensely.

The scene of a sudden car accident rarely held anything more than a little residual energy. The person's spirit didn't hang around waiting for his or her friends to show up.

"Okay," Jared said when I was done explaining all this to him. "We need a place Adam was emotionally connected to. We'll go to his house."

"I thought Avery said his family moved?"

"They did. We'll wait until the new owners are away, then we'll get in through a window or something and—"

"No! I'm not breaking into someone's house!"

Jared looked me right in the eyes. I'd never really noticed his eyes before. They were a cloudy kind of blue, but hollow somehow.

"You don't know what it's been like," he said softly. "Ever since the accident, my life has been a living nightmare. It's like I died, too, that day. I can't make it right, but with your help I know I can make it better."

It was such a heartbreaking plea. I could hear the desperation in his voice, the weight of his grief. I wanted to help him, but I knew it was probably useless. I didn't want to get his hopes up only to find nothing. It would be worse, I thought, to believe you were so close but not find the answers you were looking for. I'd seen people become fixated on reaching their dead loved ones. They would spend hours every day trying to capture EVPs on their digital recorders. It was a dangerous obsession, one that sometimes triggered strange and powerful energy that could quickly grow beyond someone's control.

"I wish I could help you," I said, returning Jared's gaze. "I really do. But it's not that clear or simple. Adam's gone, and there's no reason to think otherwise."

"You're wrong, Charlotte. And I'm not leaving until you agree to help me."

We were getting nowhere, and I didn't know what to do. I tried to think of a compromise while he stood staring at me. Then the doorbell rang.

"It's Avery!" I hissed. "You've got to get out of here."

The doorbell rang again. "Follow me," I whispered. Jared nodded, and I knew he was just as scared of Avery seeing him as I was.

Shane was still working in the living room. He had his headphones on, so I doubted he was even aware that Jared was in the house. I tapped him on the shoulder and he pulled his earphones off.

"Hey, kid? Who's your friend?"

"This is Jared. Can you give him a ride home? It's a long story, but I'll explain later. Use the back door!" I added as I ran to the foyer.

I waited as Shane and Jared left the house. The doorbell rang a third time and I opened the door.

"Finally!" Avery said as she walked in. "What were you doing?"

"Bathroom," I said, hoping the answer would suffice. It did. Avery went into the dining room and sat in the exact same spot Jared had just occupied.

"So, what's up? You said you needed to talk to me about something. Sounded important."

"It is. Kinda." I relaxed a little when I heard Shane's van pulling out of the driveway. I grabbed the channel guide from where Mom had left it on the end table and handed it to Avery.

"Hey! I've seen this show." She chuckled. "They look like your parents."

"That's because they *are* my parents."

Avery frowned. "Oh."

I apologized for not telling her sooner and gave her my rationale—that I didn't want her to think I was weird—and said that I hoped she would understand.

"In the past, it's been a problem for some people," I explained. "I was worried how you might see me."

I sat down and waited for her to say something. She just stared at the channel guide. "I knew they looked familiar," she murmured. Finally, she tossed the magazine aside and looked at me.

"Anything else? Any more deep dark secrets I should know?"

Her tone took me by surprise. I couldn't tell whether she was being sarcastic or not.

"No. That's about it."

"Okay, then. We're even. I didn't tell you something and you didn't tell me something, and that's it. I need to get home now."

She stood up and walked to the foyer. I followed her, my stomach twisting. I didn't want her to leave this way. I wanted to be sure that she would come back.

"Avery, please don't be upset."

She had her hand on the doorknob. "I'm not upset," she said as she opened the door. "It's not a big deal, okay? I'll see you on Monday morning." She smiled a little too brightly and left. I watched her walk down the street to her house, hoping that she would turn around and wave or something, but she didn't.

A little while later, Shane returned from dropping off Jared. He went to the kitchen, and I followed.

"Poor kid," he said, grabbing a beer from the fridge.

"What did he tell you?"

Shane popped open the can and sat at the counter. "Everything. His accident. His life. What he asked you to do."

I sighed. "I can't contact Adam. You know that."

"Yeah, I know. But you don't have to find his friend. You just have to try."

"Why should I try when I know it won't really help?"

Shane folded his hands together. "Because trying *would* help, Charlotte. This kid needs to know that he did everything he possibly could. I know it's not something we usually do, but after talking to him, I think it's worth a shot."

I raised an eyebrow. "I think my parents would disagree."

"Maybe." Shane shrugged. "Maybe not. Look, your parents spend a lot of time trying to release energy so it moves on. Don't you think it's even more important to help people do the same thing?"

"Mom and Dad don't see it as something moving on. They see it as balancing the energy fields of the universe."

"Fine. Then let's say that Jared's energy needs balancing."

Shane outlined a plan for me. He said I should take the thermal camera and a digital recorder from my room, spend a few hours with Jared and basically talk him through the process.

"Show him that you tried but it's not working. Tell him he needs to find a new way to deal with this. Suggest counseling. Better yet, find a way to get him to talk to your friend Avery."

"Ha. He tried that at school and Avery almost had him arrested."

"That's too bad. They could probably use each other for support." Shane stood up. "Your folks will be home late tonight. They're at another meeting." He winked.

"A psychic?"

"She prefers the term 'occult specialist,' I think." He slid a piece of paper across the counter to me. "Just in case," he said as he took his beer into the living room and returned to his computer.

I picked up the slip of paper. There was a number written on it and the words *Call him* scrawled in Shane's scratchy handwriting.

Jared's phone number.

I put the paper in my back pocket and retreated to the dining room. Maybe I would call him, but not tonight. I'd had enough conversations about talking to the dead for a while. Instead, I flopped down on the sofa and grabbed the remote control. There was never anything good to watch, especially on a Friday night, when most normal people were out with their friends.

After thirty minutes of watching overexcited hosts push their products on infomercials, my mind wandered.

If I decided to help Jared—and I wasn't absolutely sure that I would—we would need a place that had been special to Adam. His former house could be a good site, but I wasn't going to break the law on the slight chance that the place might hold residual energy. I needed someplace more public.

"You hungry?" Shane called from the living room. "I can order a pizza."

"No, thanks," I hollered back. I wasn't in the mood for pizza. The only good place to go was Giuseppe's, and they didn't deliver. The thought of their pepperoni made my mouth water, though.

It also gave me an idea. Giuseppe's was a public place, one that held happy memories for Adam and Jared and just about everyone else at Lincoln High.

I pulled Jared's phone number from my back pocket. Maybe I would take Shane's advice. I just had to make sure that Avery didn't find out, and to do that, I would need help.

I smiled. I knew the perfect person.

fourteen

I could see a woman in a long, pale dress walking down a crowded sidewalk. She held the hand of a small girl who kept turning to look at the horse-drawn carriages clopping down the street.

"Are we almost there, Mother?"

The woman nodded. "Almost, sweets."

"Why couldn't Papa come with us today?"

"He had business to attend to in town. We will see him later."

They turned at a side street. Charlotte Pickens paused, her gaze drawn to a little park. "Do you see that big tree?" she asked her daughter. "It has been there for a long, long time."

"Longer than me? Longer than you?" the little girl asked. She had the same dark hair as her mother, but her eyes were also dark, like her father's.

Charlotte laughed. "Longer than any of us. It was the only

thing standing after the great earthquake. That makes it a very special tree."

They arrived at a familiar house and rang the bell. While they waited on the porch, Charlotte smoothed her daughter's hair and patted her own locks, which were pulled back in a tight bun.

An older woman answered the door. "May I help you?"

"Good afternoon. I am here to call on Mr. and Mrs. Pickens."

"I see. Are you family?"

Charlotte hesitated. "I am an old friend," she said. "Of their daughter's," she added quickly.

"Do come in." The old woman ushered them inside to a sunny parlor. "Would you like some tea?"

"Tea would be lovely. Thank you."

The woman left the room and returned a moment later holding a silver tray. "I'm afraid the Pickenses are not here," she said as she poured the amber-colored drink into tiny white cups.

"Do you have any idea when they will be back?" Charlotte asked. Her daughter fidgeted and looked around the room, which was decorated with heavy velvet drapes and oil paintings depicting forest scenes.

The old woman sat down in a plush red chair. "They left nearly a year ago," she said. "They send telegrams once in a while. I maintain the house for them."

Charlotte set her teacup down. "A year ago? Where did they go?"

"You said you were an acquaintance of their daughter?" The woman sipped her tea.

"Yes. I was a close friend."

"They went searching for her, you know. Poor souls believe

she's still alive. They've been traveling across the North. I imagine they'll head west soon."

Charlotte nodded. When she raised her own teacup to her lips, her hand shook slightly.

"I can tell Mr. and Mrs. Pickens you were here, of course, but I don't think they will return for a while. You said your name was—?"

Charlotte stood up, and her little daughter did the same. "That's quite all right. Thank you for your hospitality."

As they left the house, the little girl began to skip. "That was a pretty place," she said. "Can we go back there?"

"I hope so," Charlotte replied, looking back. "I certainly hope so."

I awoke on Saturday morning with the dream fresh and heavy on my mind. Charlotte Pickens had returned to Charleston, but her parents had not. I guessed that her little daughter was about six years old, which meant that less than a decade had passed since Charlotte had run away.

The real question I had, though, was why I was having these dreams to begin with. If the spirits of her parents were the ones now following me, how was it that I could see Charlotte's actions? It made more sense to me that I would see her parents, that they would somehow show me their own experience of searching for their lost daughter. I wanted to trust that these dreams were authentic and were being given to me as a bizarre gift to help me understand what had happened a hundred years ago. But who was giving them to me?

After folding my blankets on the sofa, I went to find my parents. I hadn't heard them come in the night before, but Dad's keys were sitting in their usual place on the foyer table. No one was in the living room and the computer monitors were off. The coffeemaker hadn't been started, either. Usually my parents were up at six and working. They were natural morning people, which I thought was actually very unnatural. Humans were not made to jump out of bed at the crack of dawn, smiling and ready to go.

I made the coffee and went upstairs. My parents' bedroom door was open slightly, so I peeked inside. They were both asleep. The clock on their nightstand read 9:30. It must have been a late night, I thought. They never slept in so long.

I took a hot shower. When I went to my room still wrapped in a towel, I remembered that Shane had set up cameras in there. So I went back downstairs, grabbed a clean pair of jeans and a T-shirt from the folded stack sitting on the dryer, and returned to the kitchen.

Mom was sitting at the counter in her bathrobe, sipping from her favorite mug. "Thanks for making the coffee, hon," she said drowsily.

"No problem." I slid two slices of raisin bread into the toaster. "What time did you guys get home last night?"

She yawned. "Around three, I think. Poor Shane. He was asleep at the monitors."

"Three in the morning? Wow. Isn't that the time I should be sneaking in?"

She pointed a finger at me. "Don't even think about it."

I sat across from her and buttered my toast. "So where were you?"

"We went to see someone about your situation." She took another sip of coffee. "I think we have a solid plan now. Your father isn't too thrilled, but he tends to be cynical about things like this."

Mom explained that when we finally located the graves of Charlotte Pickens and her parents, we would need to perform a kind of "releasing ceremony." It involved some chanting and prayers, but the most important aspect of it was that we needed to form a "Circle of Seven."

"Seven people who believe in what they're doing and can focus," Mom said. "They join hands, recite the prayer, and hopefully, the spirits will be able to let go and join their daughter."

"Sounds sort of cheesy," I admitted. "I can see why Dad is skeptical."

"Yes. But this woman we met with, Beth, seemed sincere to me. I believed her, and you know how rare it is for me to trust someone who claims to have that kind of knowledge." Mom looked at me. "She said I should ask you more about your dreams. She said you would be having one very soon."

I almost choked on my toast. "I had one last night."

Dad shuffled down the stairs and went straight for the coffee. "Good morning."

"Charlotte had another dream last night," Mom said.

Dad froze with his hand on the coffeepot. "Did you tell her about the psychic?" He grimaced when he uttered the word "psychic," as if it was painful to say.

"Yeah. She told me." I described my dream to them. Mom grabbed a notepad and jotted down what I was saying while Dad simply listened and nodded.

"Interesting. Your previous dream may be more helpful to us, though. Annalise e-mailed a list of young men who went missing during the earthquake," he said. "We can narrow the list down by age, but this accent you mentioned may be a useful clue. We can look for foreign-sounding names."

"And if Charlotte Pickens married this guy, she would have taken his last name. We can trace them that way." I was starting to get excited. We were taking a giant step toward solving the mystery.

While Dad was printing off Annalise's e-mail, I tried to get more information from Mom about the psychic. "Did she say why I was having the dreams? Because I don't get it. It's like Charlotte Pickens is putting them in my head, but if she is, then she must be here with her parents, right?"

"Beth had a theory," Mom said slowly. "I don't know if I necessarily agree with her, but she thinks you are somehow serving as a connection between the energies involved. The girl's energy is trying to reach her parents through you and vice versa. It doesn't mean the girl is anywhere nearby, only that because her parents are nearby, she can connect to you."

"So everybody's using me," I muttered as I took my plate to the sink and rinsed off the toast crumbs. I thought briefly of Jared asking for my help and Shane telling me it was important to aid the living. By the time this was all over, I would have helped enough people to earn some kind of Girl Scout badge. I almost laughed out loud at the thought of a little round badge decorated with a ghost.

"Here's the list of males missing after the earthquake," Dad said as he came back to the kitchen. "Let's see. Only fourteen names, so that's good." He ran a finger down the paper as Mom looked over his shoulder. Most of the names sounded old-fashioned to me and not at all foreign. There were a lot of Fredericks and Franks and Walters on the list. "Alanzo de Paula," Mom said, and we all knew immediately that was the one.

"Maybe that's why her parents disapproved," I suggested. "He was a recent immigrant or something, and they wanted her to marry someone else."

"That's certainly possible," Mom agreed. "We need to re-search this last name, check records and vital statistics. I'll see what I can do."

While my parents planned a trip to the research library, I turned my attention to my backpack, which was propped against the sofa and bulging with all the homework I had to finish. I had no weekend plans, which was slightly depress-ing. I opened my British Lit text and began reading, feeling content to be doing something so perfectly normal.

I sat cross-legged on the sofa and tried to concentrate on my English assignment. I realized that I'd been spending a lot of time in the same spot. It was where I completed homework, watched TV, snacked and slept. If we left energy behind in places where we spent the most time, then I was in the pro-cess of creating a haunted sofa. Maybe one day my parents would sell it at a garage sale and some poor, unsuspecting buyers would take it home and feel my presence sitting next to them.

Halfway through writing a response to an incredibly boring poem written in a form of English I could barely understand, my cell phone rang. It was Callie.

"I need to ask you something," she said, sounding breath-less. "There's a rumor that your parents are, um, some kind of Ghostbusters."

"Well, that didn't take long." Less than twenty-four hours, I thought. A new record.

"It's true?"

I shut my lit book. "Yes, it's true. But they prefer the term 'paranormal investigators.'" I explained everything as best I could and gripped my pen as I waited for a reaction.

"Wow. That's pretty cool, Charlotte. I mean, you're kind of a celebrity."

"No, I'm *not* a celebrity," I protested. "More of an oddity. Callie, I don't want people making a big deal out of this. It can get really weird really fast." I paused. "How'd you find out?"

"I got a text. Someone saw a TV guide thing, and it's all anyone is talking about."

"Wonderful," I muttered.

"It's not a bad thing! Seriously, people think it's great."

"Right. It'll be great until after Halloween. Then they'll start trying to figure out what's wrong with me."

"You're obviously not seeing the big picture, but if you want us to downplay it, we will. Just say the word."

"The word."

Callie sighed. "Fine. But you're missing out on an incredible opportunity to be known as the greatest thing our school has seen since one of the alumni made it onto a reality dating show."

"I'll live with the regret," I said. "By the way, have you spoken to Avery today?"

"No, she's not answering her phone. Does she know yet?"

"I told her yesterday. She didn't seem too happy about it."

Callie's line clicked and I knew she had another call coming in. "Avery takes time to adjust to things," she said quickly. "She'll be fine. See you Monday."

I said goodbye and lay on the sofa. Everything had changed right when I was beginning to enjoy the life I had established. I liked my friends and my anonymity and even my class schedule. The day before, people saw me as a regular senior girl. How would they look at me on Monday?

I thought about calling Annalise for a little moral support, but I already knew what she would say. "Who cares what other

people think? Don't let the opinions of others define you."
Annalise had always been so sure of who she was, and her
confidence seemed to draw people to her, people who didn't
care that she walked into abandoned buildings as chum and
called out to the energy that resided there. She confronted
rumors head-on with a smile, while I pretended not to hear
what people were whispering.

It was strangely simple the way that one thing suddenly
defined you to other people. One day you're a normal person,
and the next you're that girl whose parents hunt ghosts. People
always tended to sum up others in just a few words, as if those
meaningless descriptions defined them forever. You were the
"shy girl" or the "obnoxious guy," and no matter what you
did, you were trapped inside the way other people chose to
see you.

I wondered if that was part of the reason why Charlotte
Pickens ran away from home. Maybe her parents had always
seen her as the "good girl" and she couldn't bear for them to
see her as anything else, especially as an unwed mother. Whatever had been her ultimate fate, I was going to find out.

Soon.

fifteen

I heard two quick honks of a car horn at exactly seven-thirty and felt relieved, as if I'd been holding my breath underwater for too long.

"Avery's here!" I yelled out to Mom and Dad. They were at their computers. "See you later!"

Mom walked with me to the front door. "We may not be here. We're going to a research library near Charleston, but we should be back before dinner."

I told her to have fun and walked out to Avery's car, a tiny knot of nervousness gnawing at my stomach. I wasn't sure what to expect from everyone at school, but I was more anxious about how Avery would treat me. Would she act aloof and irritated? Or had she decided that my family's tiny slice of strange celebrity was no big deal? I opened the passenger door and slid in, determined to stay upbeat and hope for the best.

"Good morning!" I said, then immediately cringed. I had squealed like an overexcited toddler.

Avery laughed and backed out of the driveway. "Well, you're happy today."

"Just happy to see you, I guess. I tried calling you over the weekend."

"I was busy. Spent a lot of time on the computer, actually, catching up on stuff."

Avery didn't seem angry or uncomfortable in any way, so I relaxed a little and settled into my seat. I was surprised when, instead of taking the long way to school, she turned left onto Main Street. I was going to say something but decided to let her bring it up if she wanted to.

"I'm sorry if I rushed out on you Friday," she began. "I was just taken aback, is all. It's not your parents' career—it's that you had a secret. You understand, right?"

"I understand."

We stopped at a red light. "Don't worry about today," Avery said. "You might get some stares, but it should be fine." She turned toward me, but her gaze was focused on something out my window. I turned my head as well and immediately saw what she was looking at: a short white cross near the side of the road. I'd seen it before but never made the connection.

"That's where Adam died," Avery murmured. I wasn't sure what to say. The car behind us honked, and we both looked up. The light had changed.

"Avery, I'm really—"

"You know why I never go to your locker?" she interrupted.

"No."

"Adam's locker was the one right next to yours, closest to the drinking fountain. After he died, people taped cards to it and placed flowers there. The administration decided to leave it empty this year. I wonder whose locker it will be next year."

I wasn't used to Avery rambling like this. Her tone remained casual, as if we were discussing homework or the weather, but something was off. Why was she telling me any of this, especially now? I squirmed in my seat, unsure how to respond.

"Avery, are you okay?"

"I'm fine," she said brightly. "Just being open and honest. That's what we need to be from now on, right? Open and honest."

"Right. From here on out, no more secrets."

Even as I said it, I felt guilty. I hadn't told her about Jared's visit or how I planned to help him.

We arrived at school early. Avery pulled into her parking spot but didn't get out of the car. "You're one of my best friends," she said. "I hope you know that."

I nodded. "Thanks. I do know that. And you're one of mine."

I didn't tell her that I'd never had a best friend before. My family had always moved so much, there was never any time to establish lasting friendships. Avery and I had bonded almost immediately, something that had never happened to me before.

We walked into school together, and before long the empty hallways began to fill up with students and noise and the general morning rush. Some of the other girls gathered around Avery's locker and we chatted about our weekends. Callie had obviously told them not to ask about my parents, but I could tell from the quick glances they were sharing that they were dying to ask me. Finally, I told them that it was okay.

"I know everyone has seen the channel guide," I said. "It's

fine if you want to talk about it. I just don't want it to be the *only* thing we talk about, you know?"

Callie was the first to ask me something. "So how many actual ghosts have you seen?" We were heading to first period in our usual group formation. I knew people were staring at me, but for once it didn't feel so strange. I felt protected in a way, because I was surrounded by my friends.

"Actual ghosts? The kind that look like people and float around?" I smiled. "None, unless you count the ones I've seen in movies."

I explained that most "ghosts" appeared as dark shadows or blurry shapes, not the full-bodied apparitions people expected to see. "It's more common to hear things, or see an object move, or get a really cold feeling," I went on. "It's pretty boring, actually. You can wait hours and hours for something to happen, only to get a few seconds of activity."

Trying to clarify my dad's theory about residual energy proved to be more difficult. My parents probably investigated a hundred cases a year, and out of those hundred, they usually proved that over half weren't hauntings at all but instead very simple problems involving bad wiring or faulty cables or something. They always discovered a few dozen cases of residual energy, some more complex than others.

We arrived at Doc Larsen's English class. Half the girls went one way and half the other. Callie and I took our seats and waited for the bell to ring.

"I saw a ghost once, in my grandmother's attic," Callie whispered. "It was like you described—a blurry shape moving across the room. It freaked me out. Don't you get scared?"

I shrugged. "Not really. When you grow up around stuff like that, it becomes normal."

Even as I said it, I knew it wasn't the entire truth. Certain things felt normal to me, like the sound of footsteps on empty stairs or doors opening by themselves. But when it came to the energy of the Pickenses, I felt as if I'd been thrust into the middle of something new and different. I knew if I thought about it too much I would be downright terrified.

The rest of the morning went by quickly. More people than usual said hi to me in the hallways, but only a few stopped talking entirely when I walked by. Any time I caught people looking at me, I smiled and said hello. No avoidance, I told myself. Just look them in the eyes.

By the end of the day, I felt like a seasoned pro in the art of polite nodding and smiling. I wasn't even fazed when I arrived at the AV room and a gaggle of overeager freshman boys swarmed around me. They asked questions about exorcisms and UFO sightings and anything even remotely supernatural. One kid even took notes. I just smiled and told them to read one of my parents' books.

I had been looking forward all day to seeing Noah. He was the person I wanted to help me with my plan for Jared, and I needed to talk with him. Before I could, though, Mr. Morley stopped me.

"I had no idea that your parents produced their own television series!" he exclaimed. "Think you could convince them to come in and speak to the class?"

I knew Mom and Dad would be thrilled with an invitation to my school, but the thought of them roaming the building and attracting attention was a little too much for me at the moment.

"Maybe," I said. "I'll have to ask them. They're really busy."

Mr. Morley nodded. "Of course. Well, let me know soon, okay?"

He returned to his desk while I headed toward the editing monitors. I could see Noah already working at our station, but before I could reach him, I was stopped again. This time, it was Bliss.

"What was that about?" she demanded. I was almost blinded by her bright orange blouse. She'd paired it with a green skirt, so she kind of resembled a carrot.

"What do you mean?" I was feeling impatient to see Noah, but then I realized this was a perfect opportunity to face another problem I had been avoiding: talking to Bliss for the first time since the hallway incident.

"Why were you talking to Morley? Wait, let me guess. You were trying to convince him that I should interview you, right? Since you think you're *such* a big celebrity and all?"

I sighed. "No, Bliss, I was not trying to get an interview. Actually, I'd prefer that people just dropped it."

She narrowed her eyes. "Reverse psychology doesn't work on me, Charlotte."

"How about logic? Does that work on you?"

She shook her head in disgust and stomped off. I had planned on apologizing to Bliss for something, but suddenly I couldn't remember what. She made things so difficult. At least we were speaking, although part of me questioned whether or not that was a good thing.

Finally, I was able to take my seat next to Noah at one of the monitors.

"What are we editing today?" I asked.

"The usual earth-shattering news," Noah responded. "Football scores and a French Club bake sale. What was Bliss mad about this time?"

"The usual earth-shattering issues. She's still convinced that I'm trying to steal the spotlight."

We went to work, but Noah was quieter than usual, and it began to bother me. Finally, I said something.

"Aren't you going to ask me about it?"

He didn't take his eyes off the screen. "Ask you about what?"

"I think you know. In fact, I think the entire town knows."

"I figured if you wanted to talk about it, you would. Besides, I've known since the first week of school."

"What?" I was shocked. Noah had never even hinted that he was aware of what my parents did for a living.

"My mom is a huge fan. She has all of the *Silver Spirits* books and DVDs. I sort of recognized you."

"Why didn't you say anything?"

Noah looked at me. "Like I said, I figured if you wanted to talk about it, you would."

I kind of liked the fact that he had known all along. He had never treated me differently, and now I knew he never would. "So your mom's a fan, huh?"

He chuckled. "You have no idea. She even bought one of those 'Doubt' T-shirts online."

I groaned. "I bet she'd really love our van, then."

"I don't watch the shows like she does, so I don't understand all of it, exactly. But basically, you guys don't believe in ghosts, right? I mean, your parents try to prove that they're not real."

"Right. They think that strange things are caused by different forms of energy that people leave behind."

Noah nodded. "Residual energy. So they don't believe in intelligent energy? The kind that can think and communicate and cause things to happen?"

I wondered briefly if Noah had any clue about what was

happening at home. There was no way, though. No one beyond my family knew anything about the Pickenses.

"They haven't been able to completely disprove intelligent energy," I admitted. "They don't truly believe in it, though. They think there are explanations for everything, and they just haven't discovered those explanations yet."

"But what if the explanation is that ghosts really exist?"

"Then I guess they'll need to rewrite some of their books."

Noah laughed and we left it at that. We worked on editing news footage for a while before I remembered that I needed his help with my plan for Jared.

"Hey, thanks for finding that article for me," I began.

"Did it help?"

"Sort of. But now I have more questions, and I need a favor from you."

"Another one? How many is that now?"

"I owe you, I know. Maybe an autographed book for your mom?"

He shook his head. "I was kidding. What do you need? I'm at your service."

"The article mentioned that Jared's car swerved suddenly. Did the police ever figure out why?"

Noah leaned back in his chair. "No. But there were a lot of theories floating around. Some other kids witnessed the accident. One guy swore he saw something in the road and that Jared was trying to avoid hitting it."

"Something in the road?"

"Yeah, like a squirrel or something."

Jared had told me he couldn't explain what happened. *I promised Adam I wouldn't,* he'd said. It was a promise he had kept, but he needed to break it to clear his name. *It's the*

*only way I can move on, and the only way I know to help Avery
do the same.*

"What are you doing this weekend?" I asked Noah.

"No big plans. You?"

"I'm working on something important, actually. And I
could really use your help."

"I'm all yours."

I smiled. "You may regret saying that."

Avery gave me a ride home after school. She seemed happier
than she had in a long time, which only added to my guilt
later that night when I pulled out the piece of paper Shane
had given me and dialed Jared's number.

"I'm going to help you," I told him. "But you have to do
exactly what I say."

"Anything," he said, and I could hear sad relief in his voice.
"Just name it."

"Good. First, you need to come back to school."

"What? Why?"

"No questions. We'll work on contacting Adam this weekend, but only if you're at school for the rest of the week."

Part of "operation help the living" included making sure
that Jared graduated. I didn't know how he was spending his
days, but I guessed it included sleeping too much and obsess-
ing about the past. That wasn't a life, I decided.

Jared wasn't happy, but he was back in class on Tuesday.
He didn't acknowledge me, which was good because I didn't
want Avery to know anything was going on. She was turning a corner, I thought. She was laughing more and seemed
relaxed. I wondered if it was because she was no longer carrying around the weight of her secret.

As I made more phone calls to put my plan into action, I had no idea that just down the street, Avery was working on plans of her own.

sixteen

The dream was foggy and I had a difficult time seeing Charlotte Pickens as she stood near the railing of a large ship, looking out over a dark, vast ocean. She was dressed entirely in black, and a cold wind whipped at her long dress and damp hair. Her daughter, also dressed in black, stood next to her. I tried to get a closer look at them. The daughter appeared much older than when I had last glimpsed her. I guessed that she was at least thirteen. They were speaking to one another softly, but I couldn't make out their words. I felt as if I was being pulled away from the scene by firm hands.

"Focus."

The voice was close, a strong whisper in my ear. I felt warm and comfortable, and I snuggled deeper into my blankets, relishing the sensation of sleep but aware that I was almost awake.

Charlotte stumbled as the ship rocked, and her daughter put a hand to her mother's arm.

"Are you feeling ill?" her daughter asked.

"I am fine." Charlotte tried to smile, but her face appeared pale and strained. She was not well, I thought. The dream began to fade, the images rippling like water. The scene changed again, and I could see a girl standing in front of a large tree. I recognized her as Charlotte's daughter, only she was even older than she had been on the ship, possibly in her twenties. She held a small vase in her hands. As the image became weaker, I could see her reaching into the vase. She carefully sprinkled something around the base of the tree.

"You *must* focus."

The voice was louder now. It was Charlotte Pickens, I realized. The dream was slipping away, and I opened my eyes, groggy and confused. It was pitch-black in the dining room, and when I rolled over on the sofa to look at the clock, I saw that it was almost three in the morning.

"Great," I muttered. I had stayed up late to finish a grueling precalculus assignment and had been asleep for less than two hours. I sat up and pushed the hair out of my face. My eyes felt heavy, I was thirsty and part of me just wanted to fall back into my nest of warm blankets on the sofa, but I knew my parched throat would keep me awake. Pulling a blanket around my shoulders, I shuffled to the kitchen.

Someone had left a light on, which made it easier to find the fridge. I blinked as I opened the door and an even brighter light hit my eyes. I grabbed a bottled water from the bottom shelf and shut the door. When I turned around, it seemed as if every lamp in the house had been turned on. My first thought was that my parents had come downstairs.

Then I saw where the light was coming from.

I gasped. Standing a few feet in front of me were two figures. They weren't the pale pillars I'd seen on the monitor months ago. Instead, they looked more human. I could make out their heads and shoulders, but not their faces. Fear seized me and I gripped my water bottle so tightly I thought my cold fingers would crush right through it.

I took a step backward at the same moment the taller figure moved forward. I was having trouble breathing. I wanted to scream—*needed* to scream—but I felt like stone. I couldn't take my eyes off the hazy white figures standing in front of me.

They were coming for me.

My panic was growing, and I forced myself to take a step to the side, reaching out to the counter for support. If I didn't hang on to something, I was going to pass out. My hand touched the cold granite of the countertop and I flinched, causing a frying pan to crash to the ground. The shorter figure turned and glided away from me, through the kitchen wall. The clatter when the pan fell to the floor was loud enough that I knew my parents had heard it.

The taller figure remained close to me. It moved a little, and I could see that it was extending an arm toward me. I closed my eyes and screamed. I screamed with everything I had inside me, pushing past the fear and the parched throat and even my need to breathe. I just kept screaming until my parents came running down the stairs and into the kitchen.

"Charlotte!" Mom gripped my shoulders and I fell into her arms.

"What happened? What's going on?" Dad sounded as panicked as I felt.

"They were here," I sobbed. "They were right here in the kitchen."

Mom ushered me into the dining room while Dad searched the entire downstairs, flicking on lights and opening closet doors. I sank into the sofa. Mom kept her arm around me, which I appreciated. I never wanted to be alone again.

It took me a while to calm down, catch my breath and look at my parents. Mom stayed next to me and Dad knelt by the sofa. I explained everything, starting with my interrupted dream.

"Charlotte Pickens was on a boat with her daughter," I said. "It looked as if they were going to a funeral. She was showing me what happened, but I couldn't focus. It was like we had a weak connection."

I described the figures in the kitchen, which wasn't difficult since the image was permanently seared into my brain. "Bright white," I said. "But kind of wispy, like they were made of clouds."

"Did they say anything?" Dad asked.

"Nothing I could hear." I closed my eyes. "But they definitely wanted something from me."

I was so tired, but at the same time, completely wide awake. I wondered if I would ever sleep again. *Not in this house,* I thought, leaning my head on Mom's shoulder.

"They've become so powerful," Mom said. "I think we should stay at a hotel for a while."

"They'll follow me," I mumbled.

Dad patted my hand. "Not necessarily. I still think this energy is connected to a place, that it draws from it. The longer it's here, the stronger it becomes."

I let my parents discuss the options. Their voices were soothing, and I could hear Mom's heart beat through her robe. I was warm and safe, a feeling I didn't want to lose. When Mom shifted a few moments later, I felt a flash of fear and opened my eyes.

"Not going anywhere, honey," Mom reassured me. "Just getting comfortable. Would you like some water?"

I nodded and Dad got up. "I'll get it."

"Why did this happen?" I asked Mom, feeling wide awake once more. "I mean, there were no triggers, not one. How could they appear like that?"

"I have a theory," she said. "I think it has to do with your dream, but I could be wrong. I'm going to contact Beth later and see if she can help me make sense of all this."

"I thought you didn't trust psychics."

Mom squeezed my shoulder. "Charlotte, I'm beginning to think that we have completely left the realm of scientific explanation. I'm going to go with my gut on this one."

Dad brought me my water, which I accepted gratefully and drank in one long gulp. I had forgotten how thirsty I was, and my throat was raw from screaming.

"What time is it?" I asked.

"Almost four," Dad replied.

I groaned. "I have school in a few hours."

Mom pulled a blanket around me. "No school today. You need to rest."

Relieved, I closed my eyes. I was aware that my parents were whispering to one another, but I blocked out what they were saying. It didn't matter. What mattered was that they believed me and they were taking charge. Mom wrapped the blankets around me more tightly and got up.

"Just going to the kitchen, hon," she said. "Back in a minute."

I could hear my parents talking in the kitchen. It sounded as if Dad was trying to convince Mom of something, but she was disagreeing with him. Their voices got louder, and soon they were yelling.

"Mom?" I called.

She was at my side in a second. "Everything okay?"

I sat up. "What are you guys fighting about?"

"Nothing. It doesn't matter."

"I think she should hear this, Karen," Dad said. "If she says no, then fine. But Charlotte might be open to it."

"Not tonight, Patrick. Just drop it, please."

It was serious when they used each other's first names like that. They had my attention now. "Tell me."

"We could do an EVP session right now, while the energy is strong," Dad said, talking fast. "It could help us figure out what's going on, how it's manifesting itself like this."

Mom sighed. "Patrick, we've had enough excitement for one night."

There was no way I wanted to face my ghosts again, but I knew Dad had a point. The energy was strong and we had a good chance at contacting something. They were obviously trying to communicate with me. What if they were trying to tell me that we were on the wrong path? If we were making mistakes in our search, the Pickenses would keep getting stronger and reaching out in more terrifying ways. I was afraid to contact them, but I was more afraid of them contacting me. My parents were arguing again, so I stood up.

"I'll do it."

"Charlotte, you don't have to do anything—" Mom began.

"No, Dad's right. Let's just get this over with."

I told them that if things got crazy, we were leaving the house immediately and going to a hotel. They agreed. Dad wanted to call Shane to come over, but I said that we were doing it now before I changed my mind.

"The equipment's already in my room," I told them as we walked upstairs. "Shane set it up last week."

Mom sat next to me on my bed, one arm draped protectively around my shoulder. Dad checked out all the cameras, switched things on and grabbed a digital recorder.

"Just ask some basic questions," he directed. "Five minutes, Charlotte. That's all. Then we'll be done."

He turned off the lights, which gave me a moment of pure panic. *Five minutes,* I told myself. *Just get it over with.*

I began the way I'd seen Annalise do a thousand times. I asked if anyone was there and said I'd like to speak to them. "This is Charlotte," I clarified. "I need to know what you want from me."

"We're getting something," Dad announced. I could see the dull green glow from one of his meters and sat up a little straighter.

"Please tell us what to do," I said, trying to make my voice loud and clear. I paused, hoping that the digital recorders were picking up something. We wouldn't know until we were sitting at a computer.

"We're still trying to find your daughter," I continued. "We're looking. We need more time."

"The ion meter just spiked," Dad said. "Something's here."

Mom squeezed my shoulder. "You're doing great," she whispered.

"Where should we be looking? Do you know where your daughter went? Do you know what happened to her?"

We waited awhile. I braced myself in case we saw something or heard scratching or voices, but nothing happened. Before the five minutes were up, Dad turned on the lights.

"Battery's drained," he sighed. It happened all the time. A perfectly charged battery could die within seconds when something was present. The theory behind it was that energy needed a source to draw from in order to manifest itself.

We went downstairs. I was relieved that things hadn't gotten crazy, but I could tell Dad was a little disappointed. He lived for this kind of thing.

While my parents worked on the digital recordings in the living room, I fixed up my blankets on the sofa. The sun would be rising soon. I was exhausted, and as soon as I felt safe enough, I was going to sleep. It was Friday, I realized, and I was supposed to meet Jared on Saturday. That wasn't going to happen now. I needed to focus on the dead before I could help the living. I would call Jared later and tell him we needed to wait a few weeks.

"We've got something!" Dad called from the living room.

My parents were sitting in front of one of the monitors wearing their headphones. I grabbed a pair and sat down next to them.

"This is right after you introduced yourself," Dad explained. He clicked the mouse and I watched the screen, where I could see a spiky graph which indicated voice patterns.

Please tell us what to do, I heard myself say.

Find her, a man's voice whispered.

On the recording I began speaking again while the man was still whispering, so I couldn't make out what he was saying. Then I heard my voice again.

We need more time.

A woman's voice responded. It was not a whisper this time but almost a shout.

No!

She sounded desperate, I thought, as if a deadline was quickly approaching and there was nothing she could do. I listened to the rest of the recording and heard my questions about what we should do and where we should go. The man's voice came across again, this time louder than before.

Return.

It was a command. The man's voice held none of the desperation that the woman's did; instead, he sounded angry.

Return.

It was softer the second time, and I knew it was right as the batteries had drained from the equipment. They were using all the energy they could muster to get their message across. Maybe their appearance in the kitchen had weakened them.

We listened to the recordings a few more times before taking off our headphones.

"Where are we supposed to go?" I asked. "Return where?"

Mom rubbed her eyes. "The place we came from, I suppose. Charleston."

Dad stood up. "I'll call Annalise."

"It's not even five in the morning yet, hon," Mom said. "We can wait a few hours." She turned to me. "You need to get some rest. Don't worry, we'll be right here."

I was too tired to protest, so I went back to the sofa, curled up under my blankets and wished for dreamless sleep.

seventeen

"Hey, kid. Time to wake up."

Late-afternoon light spilled through the curtains of the dining room. My head felt foggy, as though I'd been asleep for days. Shane stood in the doorway, smiling. "Good. I thought you'd slipped into a coma."

"What time is it?"

"Almost three in the afternoon. I heard you had quite a night."

"That's an understatement." I sat up and stretched my arms over my head. "Where are my parents?"

"They went to see someone."

"The psychic?"

Shane laughed. "Occult specialist. Listen, why don't you get up and I'll make you an omelet with the works. I bet you're starving."

"I am." I dragged myself off the sofa and went to the laundry room—which had essentially become my new closet—to get changed. Then I headed upstairs to shower. My bedroom door was shut. I suddenly couldn't remember the last time I'd slept in my own bed. Was it just three months ago that I'd sat on the floor and marveled at living in a new, nonhaunted house? If I'd only known then the way my life was going to twist and turn, I'd have bolted for the door.

I took a long, hot shower and imagined all of the craziness and chaos of the night before washing off me. Then I got dressed and met Shane in the kitchen, where he was folding an extra-large omelet onto a plate.

"We'll pretend this is brunch," he said. "Dig in."

Shane knew how to cook only two things: microwave popcorn and awesome omelets. He made the omelets on special occasions, like birthdays, so I was thrilled with the treat.

"Annalise called this morning," he said as he poured me a glass of orange juice. "I told her you'd call back later."

"Mmm." I nodded and kept shoveling fluffy eggs with extra cheese into my mouth. I was ravenous, as if I'd come out of hibernation after a long winter.

"Jared called, too." Shane sounded casual as he washed a spatula at the sink. "I think he was worried when you weren't at school today that you might cancel on him. I told him we were still meeting tomorrow night."

I almost choked on a mouthful of omelet. "You what? Shane, there's no way I'm doing an investigation tomorrow. I've had enough paranormal pandemonium in my life for a while."

"Yeah, I thought you'd say that." Shane dried off the spatula and came over to sit across from me at the counter. "Do you really believe we're going to contact Adam's spirit?"

"No. But we might contact something else, and I'm not ready for that. I need to get a handle on the ghosts already invading my life."

"You sure that's your reason for wanting to bail on this?"

I stopped chewing. "Yes."

Shane nodded. "Okay. Just as long as you're not trying to run away from your problems."

I set down my fork. "What are you talking about?"

He pointed to my plate. "Keep eating. I'll talk, you listen. Just hear me out. Okay?"

I went back to devouring my eggs, knowing there was nothing he could say that would change my mind.

"My family owned a funeral home," he began, "so I've been around death for a long time. My dad used to say that it's not about the dead, it's about the living. They come first." He leaned in a little. "Charlotte, your friend Jared is hurting real bad. We can help him, but I don't think we have much time."

"He's not my friend," I said softly. "I barely know him."

"He's a guy who needs our help, kid. That's all that matters."

I finished my omelet and pushed the plate aside. "You said we don't have much time. What do you mean by that?"

"I've seen this before, more times than I'd like." Shane frowned and got a kind of faraway look in his eyes. "People can live under the weight of their guilt for only so long before they snap. I've talked to Jared. He's about to lose it."

"Last night, we picked up an EVP that said there's no more time. Do you think the Pickenses are about to snap, too?"

Shane sighed. "No clue. But if they said it, they meant it. We can help Jared on Saturday and deal with your ghosts on Sunday. How's that sound?"

"You really think I should do this?"

"I really do."

"I'll think about it." I didn't like it, but I knew Shane. If he thought it was urgent, then it was. Most of the plan was his responsibility, anyway. I basically just had to show up. Still, I wasn't completely sure about the timing.

The doorbell rang and we both looked toward the foyer. I hopped off the stool where I'd been sitting and went to answer the door. Avery was standing on the front porch holding Dante in her arms, a purple leash dangling from his neck. As soon as he saw me, he began to growl.

"How are you?" Avery asked. "When I stopped by this morning your Mom said you'd been sick all night."

"I'm feeling better," I said, noticing the sky behind her. Dark gray clouds had begun to develop and seemed to swallow the sunshine. "Looks like it's about to rain. Come on in."

Avery tethered Dante to the porch, where he began to yap at some leaves blowing through the yard. "Be good," she said to him, giving him a little pat on the head.

Shane was working in the living room, so Avery and I went upstairs. I hesitated before opening my bedroom door. Dad had taken most of the equipment out to analyze the data, but I wasn't sure how much he'd left behind.

"I haven't been in here for so long," Avery said, brushing past me and walking inside. She looked around. "What happened to the mountains of clothes?"

I quickly scanned the room for cameras, recorders or any other strange devices. Nothing. In fact, my room looked cleaner than I'd ever seen it. The bed was made, the clothes were gone and someone had discreetly covered my scratched-up nightstand with a silk scarf.

"I tidied up," I said as I sat on the edge of my bed.

Avery walked around my room and paused at the window. Outside, the trees thrashed in the wind. "Looks like it's going to be a rough storm."

"How was school?" I asked, but Avery seemed distracted. She picked up something off my dresser and held it up.

"What's this?"

I grimaced. "That's a thermal camera. My dad must have left it up here."

She turned it over in her hands. "How does it work?"

"It picks up on electromagnetic energy. It shows temperatures." I didn't know how much technical stuff she wanted to hear, but I didn't think she was really listening. She set the camera back on the dresser.

Something was definitely on Avery's mind. She was too quiet, too preoccupied. I wasn't sure what to say. Before I could ask her what was wrong, she sat next to me on the bed.

"After Adam died, I called his cell phone," she said, looking down at her hands. "I called dozens of times every day, just to hear his voice. It became a habit. Then, one day, it was turned off." She snapped her fingers. "Just like that."

"Avery, I'm so sorry."

She looked at me. "I know Jared came here. I know he asked you for help. He wants you to contact Adam, doesn't he?" There was no anger in her voice. Instead, she sounded tired, as if she was simply stating a sad fact.

"How did you know?" I asked softly.

"I saw him walking toward your house last week. I've been waiting for you to mention it."

"I didn't want to upset you."

"Are you going to help him?"

"Maybe." I almost whispered the word. It felt like a betrayal for so many reasons. I had kept a secret from Avery after I'd promised I wouldn't. I had conspired with her enemy. I had essentially demolished her trust in me.

Thunder rumbled outside and I could hear Dante barking from the porch. Avery heard him, too, and stood up. I thought she was going to leave without saying anything else, but when she reached the door she turned around.

"Jared is a murderer," she said. "And the fact that you would even consider helping him…" Her words were choked off by her tears. I sprang from the bed and went to her.

"Please, Avery. Please listen to me." I tried to put an arm around her but she pulled away. "You don't know what really happened."

"Neither do you!" she sobbed. "And Jared has no right to get another chance at talking to Adam. I want answers, Charlotte, but not from Jared. Not anymore." She wiped at her eyes. "I hate feeling this way. I hate not knowing. It's a cold, empty kind of hell."

I ushered her back to the bed, where she slumped down. She looked defeated, as though she'd given up pretending that she could deal with things on her own.

"I keep living in that moment, the last time I saw him. I keep thinking if I'd just stayed at the party, then the accident would never have happened."

"You don't really believe Jared crashed the car on purpose, do you?" I asked gently.

"I didn't, at first. But he looked me in the eye and admitted it. He said he was jealous of Adam, of his relationship with me." She sighed. "There's something else, Charlotte."

I waited, although part of me knew what she was about to say.

"The thing is, when Jared kissed me that one time? I wasn't quite so innocent. I kissed him back."

"Okay," I said slowly. "That's not the worst thing in the world."

Avery wiped a tear from her eye. "It shouldn't have happened. Adam was in Rome, I was feeling lonely and Jared was just…there, you know? Afterward, he wanted to tell Adam, but I wouldn't let him."

"Sounds like you were trying to avoid hurting Adam," I said. "I think you did the right thing. I mean, one meaningless kiss during a weak moment shouldn't ruin everything."

Avery shook her head. "It wasn't meaningless. That's the problem." She looked toward the window. A jagged sliver of lightning illuminated the black sky. "I loved Adam, but I had feelings for Jared, too. They were so much alike. But Adam had been so preoccupied with college and scholarships. It was hard for us to find time together sometimes."

"Do you still have feelings for Jared?"

"No!" Avery said fiercely. Then she looked down. "I don't know. Maybe. But there's too much I don't know. I want some answers."

"So does Jared," I said. Suddenly I knew what needed to be done. "Let's make that happen. Let's do something about it. Tomorrow."

It took me a while to convince Avery to meet with me and Jared and the others. She didn't want to be in the same room with him, let alone sit across a table from him. But I knew it was the right thing. Neither Avery nor Jared would truly be able to move forward until things were settled between them. Maybe they would never be the friends they'd once been, but they didn't have to avoid each other forever, either.

Finally, she agreed that she'd seriously think about it.

"That's it, though," she warned me. "I don't want to feel forced into doing anything."

It was the best I could do, but I thought there was a good chance she'd show up.

We went downstairs. The wind was picking up speed and rattling the windowpanes. Shane was standing at the front door, peering out the window.

"Thought I heard something," he mumbled.

I introduced Avery to Shane and they shook hands. "She might be joining us tomorrow night," I said.

He nodded. "Glad to hear it."

I gave Avery a quick hug and opened the front door. Dante immediately jumped into Avery's arms and burrowed into her chest with a whimper, startling both me and Shane.

"What is that?" he exclaimed.

Avery giggled. "This is my darling little dog. He's just scared because of the storm."

"Whew." Shane smiled. "For a second there, I thought we were being attacked by mutant squirrels." He laughed. "That would be pretty cool, actually."

We said our goodbyes and I watched as Avery walked down the hill toward her house, Dante cradled safely in her arms. As they became smaller and smaller, something occurred to me. I gasped. It was like a piece of the puzzle had slammed into place.

Adam had grabbed the steering wheel, causing the car to crash. He was trying to avoid something in the road. Something small, like a squirrel. Something he had made Jared promise not to tell Avery about just before he died.

Dante.

eighteen

I didn't sleep that night. Instead, I turned on all the lights and watched TV while Shane set up a sleeping bag in the living room.

"You can take the guest room, you know," I told him, but he just shook his head.

"If you're going to be on the first floor, then so am I," he replied. I was secretly glad. Even after Shane fell asleep and began snoring, I felt better knowing he was close by.

I called Annalise while I waited for my parents to return from their latest visit to the psychic. I knew my sister stayed up late and wouldn't mind.

"I have great news!" she squealed.

"You've located Charlotte Pickens's grave and I can get rid of my stalker spirits?"

"Oh. Well, not exactly, but we're getting closer."

"We?"

"That's my great news. I've met someone!"

His name was Mills, and he was a grad student who worked

at the library and had been helping Annalise with research. She described him as tall and lanky with glasses.

"And you know how much I love a guy with glasses." She sighed.

I did know. My sister could have dated any jock she wanted, but she always gravitated toward the shy, nonathletic guys. If she had to choose between the star quarterback or the president of the chess club, it was an easy decision. I kind of understood the attraction. I wasn't really sure what kind of guy was my type. I had been hoping that was something I could soon discover, but my time had been divided between schoolwork and the supernatural.

I let Annalise gush for a while about how smart and sweet and intense Mills was before filling her in on everything that had happened over the past twenty-four hours, starting with the ghosts in the kitchen and ending with what I'd figured out about Jared's secret.

"Wow," Annalise said when I was finished. "That's heavy stuff. Why did you let me go on and on about my new boyfriend?"

"I like hearing you happy, I guess."

"Thanks." Annalise was quiet for a moment. "Okay. Let's get down to business. I do have information for you. Got a pen?"

Mills had been searching for Alanzo de Paula but had found nothing. He had decided that, like many immigrants, Alanzo had changed his name at some point. It was a good guess, and he uncovered information about an Alan Paul, who had married a woman named Charlotte in 1887.

"Mills found property records that showed they lived in Ohio for a while," Annalise said. "And they had a daughter named Elizabeth."

I wrote down everything Annalise told me. It all seemed to fit. "What happened to them?" I asked.

"We're not sure yet. We can't find death certificates for them in Ohio, so they must have moved somewhere else."

I thought about the ship and how Charlotte and her daughter had been dressed in mourning clothes. "Maybe they went to Italy," I said. "Alanzo died first. Maybe he requested that they bury him in his home country?"

"Okay. We're on it." I could hear Annalise typing something.

"What about the parents? Do we know where they're buried?"

"Not yet. Mills doesn't think they died in Charleston."

I sighed. "So we have no idea where any of these people are, but we're supposed to bring them all together? Wonderful."

"It's not over yet. We'll figure this out. Don't give up, okay?"

I told Annalise I would try to stay optimistic, but I felt as if every time we took a step closer to solving the mystery, we ended up right back at the beginning.

A few minutes later my parents' car pulled into the driveway. I said goodbye to Annalise and told her to call as soon as she found out anything.

My parents looked completely exhausted when they walked in the door, and I realized they hadn't slept at all since the day before. Dad just nodded at me and headed upstairs while Mom collapsed next to me on the sofa.

"Rough day, huh?" I asked.

She closed her eyes and smiled. "That's one way to describe it."

"What did you find out?"

"That your father has a low tolerance for concepts that aren't based on science alone."

I laughed. "I thought you knew that already."

Mom opened her eyes and rubbed at her neck. "I thought Beth offered us real insight," she said. "She knows things, but more important, she understands things."

Mom explained that the psychic was convinced that time was running out to perform the Circle of Seven ceremony. It had to do with the Pickenses' connection to me. Beth felt that they were weakening, probably because they were using all their energy to communicate with us. If the Pickenses weren't released soon, Beth said, they might end up stuck in the living world forever.

I told Mom about what Annalise had discovered regarding the name change and how I thought Charlotte Pickens had possibly traveled to Italy with her daughter for Alanzo's funeral.

"That makes sense." Mom yawned. "I think we're on the right track."

"The Circle of Seven," I murmured. I thought about who would be a part of that circle: Mom, Dad, Shane, me, Annalise and her new boyfriend. "We still need one more," I said to Mom, who looked half-asleep. "Can Beth be there?"

"I already asked. She'll try, but she lives a few hours away," Mom murmured. "She might not be able to get there when we need her."

"Oh." I wanted to ask more, but I knew Mom needed to sleep. I got up, and she lay down. I covered her with blankets, then turned off the lamp next to the sofa.

I felt wide awake. The storm from earlier had passed through, but it was still raining lightly. I stood on the front porch for a while and hugged my arms across my chest. It felt good to breathe in the clean, earthy scent of the rain-soaked night. The streetlights cast an orange glow over the wet road, making it look shiny, and the soft, steady beat of the raindrops relaxed me.

After a while I began to feel cold and went back inside. As I was turning the lock in the door, though, there was a gentle knock on the other side. I jumped, my heart pounding, and glanced toward the dining room, where Mom was still sound asleep. I could hear Shane snoring in the living room. If I screamed, they'd probably come running. There was another light knock.

"Charlotte," someone whispered. "It's me, Jared. Open up."

I opened the door a crack. "Jared? What are you doing here?"

"Can we talk?"

I stepped onto the front porch, quietly closing the door behind me. "Are you nuts? It's after two in the morning."

Jared was soaked. He ran a hand through his wet hair, pushing it out of his face. Dark circles framed his eyes, and his skin had a gaunt look to it, as though he'd been seriously ill. He shoved his hands into his jacket and took a step back.

"I was out walking," he explained. "I didn't come here on purpose. I like to walk at night, especially in the rain, and I ended up here."

"Let's sit down," I said. I was worried about him. He looked too thin, too pale. I was half-afraid he would keel over right there on my front porch. We sat on the top step, which was only a little damp from the rain, and looked out at the empty street. I waited for Jared to speak.

"I wanted to thank you for helping me," he began. "It means a lot."

"I can't guarantee you that anything will happen tomorrow night."

He nodded. "I just want to try."

I knew he was only saying that for my benefit. Jared had high hopes for our meeting. He wanted to contact Adam so badly, and he saw this as the only possible way to unburden himself from the secret he was holding.

"I know what happened that night," I said. "I know Adam was trying to avoid hitting Dante."

Jared flinched but kept his eyes on the streetlight across from us. "How did you find out? Does Avery know?"

"No, Avery doesn't know. I figured it out on my own."

"Adam bought Avery that dog as a birthday present two years ago," he said. "I went with them to the pet store. I remember joking that we should buy a hamster wheel, too, because he was so small." He turned to me. "You can't tell her, Charlotte. She'll blame herself. She shouldn't have to feel guilt like that."

"Well, neither should you. Besides, I thought you wanted to be able to break your promise to Adam. I thought you wanted to tell Avery the truth about the accident."

He pushed back his wet hair again. "I don't know what I want."

We sat silent for a few moments. The rain was slowing down to a delicate drizzle. The houses on my street were completely dark. All the normal people were warm and asleep in their beds.

"Avery also told me about the kiss," I blurted out. "I keep hearing that you and Adam had a fight over her. Did you tell him?"

Jared shook his head. "That's not what we were fighting

about. I keep my promises, Charlotte. I never told him. I wanted to, though. Still do."

"So what *were* you and Adam fighting about that night?"

"He was going to turn down his football scholarship and go to school in town so he could stay near Avery. I told him it was a mistake. I told him—" He looked down. "I told him she wasn't worth it, that he could survive a year without her."

"Oh."

"Sounds bad, doesn't it? Especially now."

"Sounds like you were just being honest," I said.

"Yeah, well, his mind was made up. He hadn't told anyone yet, though. I was still trying to talk him out of it when we got in the accident."

We fell quiet again, but it was a comfortable kind of quiet, the kind in which you know the other person is thinking about things. I mulled over everything Jared had told me, trying to find the right words.

"I think I know what you want," I finally said.

He looked up. "What do you mean?"

"You said you didn't know what you wanted, but I think what you truly want is forgiveness. The thing is, I don't think you did anything that needs to be forgiven."

He didn't reply at first. Instead, he leaned back on the steps and continued to gaze at the streetlights. I wondered when he had slept last. The lines under his eyes made me think it had been a while.

"After I got out of the hospital, I would go to Adam's house and look up at his bedroom window. Sometimes I'd call his cell phone just to hear his voice."

I looked up. It was exactly what Avery had done. Avery and Jared had shared a strong friendship with Adam. Now they shared an even stronger grief.

Jared kept talking. "I even broke into his locker once looking for something, anything. A sign, I guess."

"What kind of sign?"

"A sign that it was his time to go. A sign that this was the way it was supposed to end."

"Did you find it?"

He smiled sadly. "Still looking."

We stayed on the porch for another hour. We didn't speak much, but it was okay. I liked sitting next to him. I kept stealing little glances at him. Despite his drawn appearance, Jared was still gorgeous. I could see why Avery had given in to her attraction for a moment. And there was something about his determination to make things right that made me want to help him. He was a good guy, and good guys were something of a rare species.

After the rain finally stopped, Jared stood up, thanked me for talking with him and began to walk home. I watched him for a while, the way he limped and kept his head down, and wished I could make things better. Maybe, I thought, the meeting with Avery would help. Maybe everything would be better by this time the next day.

Or maybe everything would become much more complicated.

nineteen

The parking lot of Giuseppe's was crowded with cars and people and waiters passing out slices of complimentary pizza. Our black van was parked in the center, the silver "Doubt" painted on its side. People gathered around it, and Shane happily posed for pictures while Mom signed a few autographs. I stayed off to the side, watching the crowd and waiting for the arrival of my friends.

Shane and Mom had worked with the owner of Giuseppe's to set everything up. The deal was that they would sign autographs and draw a crowd and, in return, we would get two hours inside the restaurant after it closed. Mom would do the talking and lead the session while Shane, Noah and I worked the equipment. Dad was at home, working on the Pickens problem, and had promised to call us if he found anything.

As the sun began to set and the crowd thinned out a little, I spotted Noah and waved to him.

"Over here!" I hollered.

Noah waved back and headed my way, followed by a dark-haired woman wearing a leather jacket and cradling an armful of books.

"This is my mom," he said when they reached me.

I was struck by how young she looked, then remembered that she had been just a teenager when she'd had her children.

"Call me Trisha," she said, smiling as she looked around at the small but noisy crowd. "This is so exciting! I brought all my books to be autographed." She turned back and looked at me. "Noah talks about you all the time. I'm so thrilled he's met a nice girl! And a celebrity, at that!"

"Mom!" Noah looked mortified. His cheeks flushed bright red and his wide eyes told me that he needed help before his mom said anything else.

"I'm not a celebrity," I said.

"Oh, I think all these people would say otherwise." She smiled at me. "Okay, I'm off to get my books signed. See you in a few minutes, sweetie." She kissed Noah's still-red cheek and moved toward the van.

"I'm sorry about that," Noah stammered, staring at the pavement. "I needed a ride and she's a really big fan. I don't talk about you all the time. She was just excited and…"

"Hey, I know all about embarrassing parents," I interrupted. "At least your mom doesn't drive around in a 'Doubt' van."

He shrugged and kept his eyes on the parking lot.

"I haven't thanked you yet for helping us out," I said, determined to make Noah comfortable again. "I'm really glad you're here."

I told him all about my visits the day before with both Avery and Jared. Noah listened, nodding at times and furrowing his brow as if he was trying to make sense of it all. Part of me wanted to open up about the Pickenses' ghosts, but I knew it would take too long.

"Sounds as though we're doing this just in time," he said when I was finished. "I mean, both of them need this, I think, in order to move on."

"But I don't want to give them false hope. I don't honestly believe anything is going to happen tonight."

"It's not false hope," Noah said. "It's hope, plain and simple. And maybe nothing will happen with Adam's energy, but something else could occur, something that *will* help Avery and Jared."

I wanted Noah to be right. I wanted to make things better for my friends, not worse. I was afraid that trying to contact Adam would result in only more heartache for both of them. As another hour passed and the crowd began to leave, a tight nervousness clenched my stomach.

Finally, Shane moved the van to a parking space next to Giuseppe's entrance and began unloading equipment. Noah and I went over to help. His mom was talking with Shane and seemed genuinely excited.

"Mom? You can pick me up in a couple of hours," Noah said.

"Oh, sweetie! Good news! Shane says I can stay and watch. Isn't that thrilling?" She looked at Shane with an adoring gaze. In return, Shane beamed, clearly loving the female attention. They were about the same age, I realized, and Trisha was pretty. She didn't look like a typical mom in her leather jacket and boot-cut jeans.

"Great," Noah muttered. He glared at Shane, who didn't notice because he couldn't take his eyes off Trisha.

I saw Avery pull into a spot at the other end of the parking lot. Instead of getting out of her car, though, she simply sat there, her hands on the steering wheel. I walked over to her car and let the others take care of setting up. I tapped on the window, startling her. "Avery?"

She opened the door but remained sitting in the driver's seat, her car keys dangling in the ignition. "Hey, Charlotte."

I squatted down so I was looking right at her. "You ready for this?"

"I don't know."

"My mom's done this a hundred times," I assured her. "Thousands, even. If anything gets too weird, she'll stop it. If you feel uncomfortable, we'll stop. But it'll be fine, I promise."

As soon as I said it, I wished I hadn't. I did not make promises lightly, and this was one I wasn't sure I could keep. It worked, though. Avery nodded and got out of the car, and we walked into the restaurant together.

The first thing I noticed was how dark it was inside. Most of the lights had been turned off, with only a few dim sconces illuminating the brick walls. After a few seconds my eyes adjusted and I led Avery toward the middle of the restaurant, where Shane was showing Noah how to operate the main camera.

"I've used one like this in class," Noah said.

Shane laughed. "Not one this nice, I'll bet. Make sure you don't push any of these." He pointed to some buttons on the side, while Noah's mother stood nearby, a giddy smile stretched across her face.

"Over here, girls!" Mom was standing in front of a corner booth across the room. Avery reached for my hand and I squeezed hers in return. When we reached the booth I saw that Jared was already there, his hands folded neatly on the table.

"Avery, I'd like you to sit across from Jared," Mom directed. "Charlotte, I want you on the thermal. You can sit right here." She pulled up a chair so that I was off to the side but still had a good view of the table.

I flicked on the camera and held it up to check the readings. Thermal cameras show temperature with color. The booth where Avery and Jared sat appeared as a dull green on my screen while Avery and Jared themselves appeared as bright red outlined with some orange and yellow. I moved the camera around to make sure that the room's overall temperature was within normal ranges. The pizza ovens glowed red on my screen, which made sense because they had been turned off less than an hour before, but there were no cold spots or anything else abnormal within the restaurant.

"Looks good," I announced.

Mom was speaking softly to Avery and Jared, telling them how the process would work. Noah was behind the main camera while Shane held an EMF reader, which he waved over the table to get a base reading of the electromagnetic field. Trisha stood directly behind him, and I caught Noah glancing over at her a few times, clearly annoyed.

After everything was set up and tested, we began. "We're here today to connect with any energy that may want to communicate with us," Mom said. She pulled up a chair and sat at the end of the booth. Avery and Jared had their eyes closed in concentration, their hands folded on the table. I hadn't seen them make eye contact or speak to one another since we'd arrived.

"Is there anyone here?"

Mom waited, knowing that the first part of the process—triggering some kind of energy—usually took the longest. We were quiet for several long minutes. The colors on my thermal camera stayed constant.

Mom spoke again, and Avery shifted in her seat. Her hands moved forward slightly, nearly touching Jared's. Suddenly, the colors on my monitor changed from red and yellow to bright orange. The orange deepened and became a shade of purple I had never seen on the equipment before.

"I think I've got something," I announced.

"Same here," Shane said. "We had a spike."

Mom nodded and whispered something to Avery and Jared. They opened their eyes, and for a split second they were looking directly at each other. Just as quickly, Avery looked away, and my monitor returned to normal.

"What's so special about this place?" Mom asked.

"We used to come here after all our games," Jared said. "We always sat here, in this booth. Adam liked it because he could see the pizza ovens from here."

Avery smiled. "He used to order the craziest combinations, like pepperoni and pineapple."

"Or tuna fish and banana peppers," Jared added.

The strange purple color was seeping back into the corners of my monitor. It was like a mist that surrounded Avery and Jared. "Keep talking," I said. "Something's happening."

Mom came over and stood behind me to look at the monitor while Jared told a story about how he had once dared Adam to eat an entire large pizza by himself.

"He just folded it like a taco and ate away," Jared said, a small smile on his face.

"I remember that," Avery chuckled. "He didn't want pizza for the next two weeks."

"Interesting," Mom murmured from behind me. She returned to the booth. "Okay, we're getting some good readings.

I want you to do something for me now. I want you to hold hands."

Avery looked shocked while Jared sat there with a pained expression on his face. Mom knelt by the booth.

"I think you can form a stronger connection by doing this. I think it will help."

Avery slowly nodded and reached for Jared's hands. They kept their eyes down, and I could tell their hands were only lightly touching. Still, as soon as they touched, purple flooded my screen.

"Another spike," Shane announced.

"I want you to close your eyes again," Mom instructed Avery and Jared. They did. "Now I want you to picture Adam in your minds. Think about the last day you saw him."

Her voice was almost hypnotic. It was calm and assured and I knew she was leading them somewhere with it. "I want you to speak directly to Adam," Mom continued. "What would you say if you knew he could hear you right now?"

Avery was the first to speak. "I'm sorry that I didn't tell you I loved you the last time I saw you." Her voice was soft. "I'm sorry I was too wrapped up in myself to think about giving you a hug or to really look at you one last time."

"But you didn't know it would be the last time," Jared said gently.

The purple color on my monitor deepened. It didn't make sense to me. I checked the sidebar to see what temperature purple represented, but in the split second I moved my eyes off the screen, the color changed again, this time to a turquoise-green. I took a step back, thinking the camera was malfunctioning and needed to be readjusted. Usually there were subtle changes, such as a light red becoming dark red.

But my monitor was going from bright orange to purple to blue, something I'd never seen happen.

"I'm sorry that I spent the last moments you were alive criticizing you," Jared was saying. I was barely listening, my attention focused instead on the thermal camera, which was beginning to show something that looked like a crazy tie-dyed design.

I moved slowly toward Shane. "I think this is broken," I whispered.

He glanced over. "Whoa. The EMF must be busted, too. These readings are all over the place."

"Now I want you to tell Adam what you want from him," Mom said. "What do you need?"

"I need to know that he's okay," Avery said. "I need to know that he understands that I love him, and that I miss him every single day. And I need him to forgive me for kissing Jared."

"I need…" Jared stopped. He seemed to be struggling with what to say. "I also need his forgiveness. And I need to be able to tell Avery about what happened that night. I promised Adam I wouldn't. I need to break that promise."

"What do you mean, you promised Adam?" Avery asked. She gripped Jared's hands, and the crazy colors on my monitor intensified. "Please tell me. I have to know."

Jared's story unfolded slowly. He hesitated at points, but he had finally revealed everything: his fight with Adam over turning down the scholarship, how Adam had grabbed the wheel to avoid running over Dante and finally how Adam's last request was to make Jared promise not to tell Avery what had really happened.

When Jared was finished speaking, he looked directly at

Avery. They were both crying. I could see the tears running down their faces, but they continued to hold hands.

"Thank you for telling me," Avery said. "I know that was difficult for you."

"I don't want you to feel guilty. It wasn't your fault."

Avery nodded and looked down but said nothing. Jared leaned in, and I could tell he was squeezing Avery's hands.

"I mean it," he said. "It was *not* your fault."

"If I'd been more careful with Dante, if I'd made sure he didn't get out of the house that day—"

"Listen to me. There was nothing you could have done. I was in the car with him, and I couldn't do anything."

Jared choked a little on his last sentence, and I wondered if it was the first time he'd said the truth out loud. Avery looked at him.

"It was an awful accident. It wasn't your fault, either. I hope you know that."

"I do now."

They looked at each other, neither one wanting to let go of the other. My screen flashed a dozen different colors before abruptly turning off by itself.

"I have no idea what just happened," I said to Mom as we moved toward a corner, "but I think it's time for a new camera."

Mom smiled. "Maybe it's just time to look at our data in a new way."

"Do you think Adam was actually here?" I asked. I looked over at Avery and Jared, who were talking to each other. "I mean, I didn't think his energy would stay behind after he died. It doesn't make sense."

"Oh, I don't think it was Adam's energy," Mom said as

she checked the thermal. "I think it was something else entirely."

Avery and Jared were still so deep in conversation that they didn't seem to notice the rest of us.

Shane came over, shaking his head. "That was messed up. I'm going to be studying the tapes for a month trying to figure this one out." He walked toward Noah and began taking down the main camera with Trisha.

"So what was it?" I asked Mom.

"Hmm?"

"You said it wasn't Adam's energy. So what was it?"

"I think it was another kind of energy. I think it came from them." She waved her hand in the direction of Jared and Avery. They were smiling at each other, and I felt a twinge of something. Not jealousy, exactly, but something about the way Jared looked at Avery, something about how *intimate* it seemed and, well, I knew I wanted that for myself. I wanted someone to gaze at me that way, someone to share a truly incredible moment with. I wondered how long I would have to wait.

Mom was still talking. "I don't know what I'd call it, but whatever it was, it was a good thing, don't you think?"

I needed a clearer answer, something more definitive than "another kind of energy." Before I could ask Mom more questions, though, the front door of Giuseppe's flung open and Dad came marching toward us.

"We have to go," he said to me and Mom. He was out of breath and his voice held a frantic edge to it. "Now."

"Patrick, what's going on?"

"Everything. Time's up. I'll explain on the way there." He looked around at everyone in the room and seemed to be counting them all. "Seven. Okay, that should work," he muttered.

Mom placed her hand on Dad's arm. "Are you okay?"

He ignored her and addressed everyone. "We need your help, all of you," he said. "We need you to come with us right now."

"Where?" Trisha asked. She was standing so close to Shane that she was almost on top of him.

"To Charleston. We have to leave right now. I'll explain on the way there." He turned to me and Mom again. "We found the Pickenses. All three of them. But there's no time left. We have to do this tonight."

"Tonight? Why?" I had never seen my dad so anxious. He looked at me, and there was something dark in his eyes. Fear, I thought. He's actually afraid.

"This is it," he said as he gathered up some of the gear. "We're almost out of time."

"How do you know?" Mom asked.

Dad was already carrying equipment toward the front door, but he paused to answer Mom's question.

"I know because they told me."

twenty

When ghosts speak, you listen. And if you don't—well, they find a way to *make* you listen.

But they don't use words.

I saw for myself what had spooked Dad so badly when we made a quick stop home before heading to Charleston. Mom said she needed her notebook, which contained all the information on how to perform a Circle of Seven ceremony. She also wanted me to wear Annalise's pink sweater.

"It worked before," she explained, "and I want to make sure we do everything we can to facilitate contact."

We pulled up to the house while Avery called her mom to tell her she'd be spending the night. Jared called his folks, too, and of course, Noah was already with his mom, who was riding shotgun next to Shane.

I was right behind Mom when she opened the front door and gasped.

"Oh, no."

"What is it?" I craned my neck to see around her.

"Stay here, Charlotte. I'll get what we need."

She went in and shut the door behind her, but I opened it a little and peeked inside. The entire downstairs looked as if it had been ransacked. Chairs had been tipped over and papers lay scattered across the foyer. I opened the door wider and took a step inside. Around the corner, jagged pieces of a lamp littered the carpet. The sofa where I'd been sleeping for the past month sat in the center of the room, strangely intact.

I wanted to check the damage in the living room, hoping that all of our computers had been left untouched by the chaos. As soon as I took a step forward, though, I felt something ram my chest. It was as if someone had shoved me with both hands. I fell backward and bumped my head on the wall.

Stunned, I looked around. Mom came running down the stairs with her notebook and the sweater. "Charlotte? What happened? Are you okay?"

"I was pushed," I said, getting to my feet. "I'm fine."

"We have to get out of here." Mom ushered me out of the house and onto the front porch. "We can't come back until this is done."

"What if something goes wrong? What if we can't perform the ceremony right?"

We reached the van and Mom pulled open the sliding door. "We'll deal with that when and if we need to," she said. "Shane, stay close to us. We'll be making one stop along the way."

We had decided to take two vehicles. Mom and Dad would drive their car and lead the way, while the rest of us would cram into the van so I could explain what was happening.

I squeezed into the seat next to Noah as Mom slammed the door shut. The very back of the van held our equipment, leaving room enough for only one row of seats. It was made

to fit three people, so Jared, Avery, Noah and I were struggling to get comfortable as Shane drove behind my parents.
I was practically sitting in Noah's lap while Jared and Avery
sat next to each other. I wanted to ask them about what had
happened at the restaurant, but it wasn't the time.

"I think there's a seat belt lodged in my back," Noah muttered, and we all laughed a little, relieved at the break in
tension.

It was dark outside. I glanced at the dashboard clock, surprised that it was already after eight. The drive to Charleston
would take two hours. It was going to be a late night.

"Um, Charlotte?" Shane was looking at me through his
rearview mirror. "I think everyone's ready to find out what's
going on."

"Oh, right." Everyone was quiet, waiting for me to reveal
the reason why we were speeding down a highway at night.
"I don't know where to begin," I said, almost to myself.

"Start at the beginning, kid. Start with the Courtyard
Café."

So that's how I began my story, with Annalise and me
walking into the Courtyard Café for the first time and all
the things that happened afterward. I included descriptions
of my dreams and tried to explain what we'd learned about
the Pickenses, and ended with being shoved inside the house.
No one said anything until I had finished.

"So these ghosts follow you around?" Avery asked. "I mean,
do you think they're here with us right now, in this van?"

"I hadn't thought about it," I admitted. We all looked
around slowly, as if we might see two pale spirits crouched
behind the seat.

"So, what do you guys think?" Shane asked. "You going
to help us?"

"We haven't given them much of a choice," I muttered.

"I'm in!" Trisha exclaimed. "This has been, by far, the most exciting day of my life!"

I turned to the others, my hair brushing against Noah's cheek as I did so. "I know I'm asking a lot. I'm asking you to believe in something that's, well, unbelievable. But I need your help."

Jared spoke first. "Charlotte, you were the only person who would listen to me when I needed to talk. If you need help, I'll do whatever I can."

"Of course I'll help," Avery said. "I don't know what happened at Giuseppe's, but I feel different. A *good* different. And it's because of you. So yeah, I've got your back."

"Me, too," Noah said. "Just tell me what to do."

I was a little overwhelmed at the thought that I was surrounded by people willing to walk into the unknown with me. It was as though I was leading them into a battle that I wasn't sure we could win. Now that the Pickenses had shown they could manifest strongly enough to cause physical damage, I was truly scared. If we failed, would they stalk me forever, throwing things around and pushing me to the ground? Or worse, would they physically harm the people around me?

A little later, Shane pulled over at a gas station and Mom walked over to the van.

"Okay. Charlotte, you're going to ride the rest of the way with your dad so he can explain what we've found. I'll ride with you guys and fill you in. I want to go over the ceremony with all of you, too."

She looked at our tight seating arrangement and frowned. Noah got up with me. "I'll just sit on the floor, Mrs. Silver," he offered.

"Thanks, hon." She gave me a quick hug. "Everything will be fine, Charlotte. This is almost over."

I jogged over to my parents' car and slid into the passenger seat. Dad was pulling away before I even had a chance to fasten my seat belt.

"Your mom says you were hurt," he said as he pulled onto the highway. His voice was hard.

"I was shoved. It wasn't bad," I said. "I think they were trying to tell me to get out of the house, you know? To return to Charleston."

Dad didn't reply. He was focused on the road, but his jaw was clenched and I knew he was angry. I stared out at the dark road stretched in front of us. There wasn't much traffic, and I found myself checking the side mirror every so often to make sure the van was still behind us. It was. I wondered what Mom was telling the others, what new information had created such urgency in my dad. He was usually so calm and scientific. Had he been attacked by the Pickenses, too?

After a few minutes, the silence became uncomfortable, so I decided to speak up. "What happened tonight?"

Dad shook his head. "I don't know. I really don't."

He said that he had been working at the computer when Annalise called with new information. She and Mills had finally found the Pickenses' graves.

"There was a mistake with their grave markers," Dad explained. "From what the records show, the Pickenses died in Wisconsin while looking for their daughter. Their bodies were shipped back to Charleston, but someone along the way misspelled their names."

"But they're definitely in Charleston? What about Charlotte Pickens?"

"That's where it gets weird."

Dad had put Annalise on the speakerphone. As she talked about the trail of paperwork they followed to find Charlotte Pickens, things started happening in the house. A lamp switched off, but Dad assumed that the bulb had simply burned out. Then Annalise said they believed Charlotte had traveled to Sicily after her husband died from pneumonia in Ohio. Dad heard the back door open and shut, and he thought that one of us had returned from the restaurant. When Annalise said that Charlotte had died in Sicily, leaving her daughter to be raised by her husband's family, everything erupted.

"It was like a tornado formed inside the house," Dad said. "The furniture moved, papers flew in the air and there was a constant pounding, as if someone was stomping their feet— but on the walls. I've never seen energy manifest itself like that."

"Do you really think this is just your typical energy?" I asked. "After everything that's happened, don't you think this is more advanced, more *human* than anything else you've studied? These are ghosts, Dad. Real ghosts."

"Honey, the definition of 'ghost' is so subjective…"

"Not to me. These were real people once, and they're more than residual energy now. We're dealing with intelligent beings here."

"You sound like your mother." I could tell by the way Dad said it that he didn't mean that as a good thing, but I was too angry to argue. How could he be so stubborn? Furniture flew at his head and he was acting as though it was just another scientific anomaly, something he could study later and pinpoint the cause.

"You told me once that something happened to you that you couldn't explain," I said. "Remember? The figure that passed in front of you and said, 'excuse me'?"

"Pardon me."

"What?"

Dad's voice was softer. "It said, 'Pardon me.'"

"Did you ever figure out what that was?"

"No. I've tried, though. I've been back to that place a dozen times."

"You also used to say that sometimes things are simply a normal we don't yet understand. So maybe we need to use a kind of approach we don't yet understand, like this Circle of Seven ceremony."

Dad seemed to mull this over for the rest of the ride. Soon, we were approaching the long bridge that would lead us straight into downtown Charleston—and toward whatever it was that waited for us there.

twenty-one

It wasn't working. We were on our third try, holding hands as Mom recited the words to the Circle of Seven ceremony, but nothing was happening. The equipment barely blinked and the room temperature in the Courtyard Café remained steady on the thermal camera. Mom flipped through her notebook, scanning for something she may have missed.

"I don't understand," she murmured. "I'm following the steps correctly."

Dad cleared his throat. "Time to go to plan B, then?"

Mom glared at him. "No, Patrick, it is *not* time to go to plan B."

Plan B, as Dad had briefly explained when we got to Charleston, was to set up every piece of equipment we owned and antagonize the energy. Sometimes, hurling insults triggered fast results. Not good results, though, and after feeling the force of what the Pickenses were now capable of, I didn't want to make them any madder than they already were.

At the moment, though, we were relying mainly on Mom's

words, my voice and a few basic devices to detect fluxes of energy as we stood in the main dining area of the café. The Circle of Seven had been holding hands tightly for the past hour, and I could tell by their wearied looks that they were beginning to lose focus—as well as hope that we were going to achieve anything.

"How about a brief break?" Annalise asked. "Some of us have to use the bathroom."

Annalise and Mills had met us at the Courtyard Café, where they had arranged for us to occupy the place for the evening. We weren't planning on being there all night, but nothing seemed to be happening.

Everyone left the room for a break except for Mom and me.

"Maybe we've already run out of time," I said miserably as I plopped down on a chair. "Maybe the Pickenses were too weak to follow us here or something."

"I don't think so," said Mom. "I think if we'd missed our window, we'd be dealing with some very angry energy right now."

I put my head down on one of the round tables. I was tired and worried and just wanted everything to be over with. I closed my eyes and let myself feel the cool white tablecloth against my cheek. "Help us," I whispered.

At that moment, I saw something clearly in my mind. It was a single, fleeting image that flashed before me in less than a second, but once I saw it, I understood the problem.

I sat up. "It's not the ceremony!" I yelled. "It's the place!"

Mom gave me a strange look and Dad came running in from the other room. I was already making my way to the door.

"We're in the wrong place," I told him. "Grab your stuff and let's go."

"What are you talking about? Where are we going?"

The others had gathered in the front room and were looking at me as if I was crazy.

"But this is where the Pickenses lived," Mom reminded me. "This is where it all began."

"Not exactly." A grandfather clock near the front door rang eleven times. I waited until the loud chimes stopped before speaking again. "Look, I need you to trust me. We're close, I promise. Just follow me."

I hoped I sounded more confident than I felt. I walked briskly and with a sense of purpose, and the others followed, talking among themselves. Outside, the streets were fairly empty and I breathed in the scent of the air, tinged with tired jasmine. It took a few minutes to reach our destination, but when we finally arrived, I knew it was the right place.

The image that had flashed before me moments earlier was that of a huge old tree. It was in the same park where the Pickenses had camped after the earthquake. It was the same place I had seen in my dreams. And, most important, it was the same tree where Charlotte Pickens's only child had returned to fulfill her mother's last request.

"The park? Are you sure?" Mom asked.

"Not the park. It's the tree." I explained what I'd seen and how it connected to everything else, but Dad wasn't so sure.

"You saw a tree. They all look alike. How do you know it's this particular one?"

I took a step forward and reached for the trunk. "I just know."

The moment my fingers touched the bark, everything went

black. I turned around, but instead of finding my family and friends, a girl stood there, smiling.

A dark-haired girl wearing a pink dress.

"You found me," Charlotte Pickens said.

I was stunned, but at the same time, it felt as if I was exactly where I was supposed to be, even though I had no idea where—or when—I was.

"I think you're the one who found *me*."

"True. But thank you for letting me in."

I looked around. It was still nighttime and we were still in Charleston, but it looked different. Smaller, somehow, like the town itself was closing in. Beyond the park it was solid black. No buildings, no trees.

"There's not much time," the other Charlotte said. "I can feel things slipping away."

"How do I contact your parents?"

"I will take care of that. I need you and your friends to focus, though. Really focus on what you are doing and why."

"The ceremony will work?"

She nodded. "It will do."

I felt as though I was in a waking dream. Was I standing in a spirit world, talking to a real ghost?

She giggled. "Yes, in a way."

"You can read my mind?" The thought was scary.

"Only here," she assured me.

I had so many questions I wanted to ask her. How many people had ever had a chance to ask a dead person what it was like after you died?

"It's different for everyone," she said. "Just like being born is different for everyone. Some things are essentially the same, but the experience itself—and what happens afterward— depends greatly on who you are."

She looked young, like the teenager I'd first witnessed running away from her parents' tent. In my later dreams, though, she had appeared to be at least ten years older.

"You can choose the form you take," she said. "I thought this would be best for my parents because it is how they always thought of me."

"Have you been stuck here all this time?"

"Yes and no. I cannot move on yet, but I can leave this place." She waved her arm at the park, which was even smaller than it had been seconds before.

"I always thought people came back to the place where they lived, not where their body was, um, well, I guess you weren't buried here, exactly, but your ashes…"

Charlotte laughed. "I asked my daughter to scatter my ashes here because it was a place I loved," she said. "I used to come here whenever I could. So, yes, it was a place where I lived, in a way. It was special to me."

"Why weren't you able to find your parents? They've been in Charleston all along."

Her face darkened. "They reside in a different kind of place. Sometimes they can hear me, but they are trapped in a way that I am not. What you are about to do—it will free them."

"Why me?" I asked. "I mean, why do they need anyone *living* to help them? And what happens if we can't?"

She sat down in the grass, her pink dress fluttering around her. "It was their choice," she said. "When they made the decision to remain behind, they imposed upon themselves their own rules, their own deadline. They did not know how powerful and binding such a decision becomes." She smiled sadly. "It is truly amazing what one can accomplish by simply focusing on it long enough."

It was getting darker. Charlotte Pickens was becoming harder to see and I still had a thousand questions to ask.

"Is it scary? The whole afterlife—is it what you thought it would be?"

She looked at me with her wide brown eyes and smiled. "It is nothing like I thought it would be. It's bigger, I suppose. More complex." Her gaze shifted to the tree, then back at me. She stood up. "It is time to go."

"This is the end?" I asked.

She laughed. "That is one thing you learn here. There is no end." She leaned close to me and whispered something in my ear. I wasn't sure what she meant, but before I could ask, she was gone. I blinked, and was once again standing next to the tree, my fingers barely touching its bark. Noah was standing next to me.

"How long was I out?" I asked.

He frowned. "Out where?"

"Didn't I just pass out?"

Noah put his hand on my shoulder. "No. Hey, are you feeling all right?"

I didn't know what I was feeling, but I knew what we had to do. "Let's get started," I said. "We need to form a circle around the tree."

We joined hands and Mom began to read from her notebook. Shane held a small, battery-powered video recorder while Dad watched the EMF reader.

"We have come here today to release the spirits of Edward and Elizabeth Pickens, to join them with their daughter and to guide them toward a new life," Mom read. I quietly repeated everything she said and tried to focus on the words.

Noah held my right hand while Annalise held my left. We were all standing with our heads bowed and our eyes closed as

Mom had told us to do. Passersby probably thought we were performing some kind of hippie tree ceremony, I thought, then quickly brushed the thought aside. I wondered if everyone else was having the same trouble concentrating as I was.

Mom kept reading, her voice soft but strong. I knew the words before she even said them. It was like a prayer with instructions. We were halfway through when I felt movement behind me. Dad was whispering something to Shane about the readings.

Focus.

I squeezed Annalise's hand and she squeezed back. "Something's happening," she breathed.

A breeze had picked up. It seemed to swirl around us, almost like the air was dancing.

"We form this circle to join our energy, to provide a space where you can connect to one another," Mom read.

I was listening to Mom but thinking about the Pickenses, too. They had searched unfamiliar places, never giving up hope that their child was alive somewhere. Would their lives have been better if they'd given up their quest and stayed home? Or would giving up have been too painful for them?

It is truly amazing what one can accomplish by simply focusing on it long enough.

I made myself listen to my mom's words. I knew she was coming to the end of the ceremony, and I wanted to focus as hard as I could on what was being said. The breeze was swirling faster, with a stronger intensity. I closed my eyes more tightly as it whipped at my face and hair.

"Enter the circle and find your daughter," Mom said. Her voice was louder, as if she was trying to be heard over the growing wind. "Find the peace you have been seeking and be released from your past."

Noah was clutching my hand so hard it hurt. I opened one eye and saw that everyone in the circle was staring at the tree. I looked up, trying to see through the hair flying around my face.

"Wow."

A pale pink ball of light glowed near the base of the tree. As the wind became more fierce, two golden lights joined it. They circled and spun and became brighter. The light grew so intense that finally I had to look down. A second later, the wind stopped completely, and when I looked up, we were standing in darkness.

No one broke the circle. No one let go of the hands they were holding. We waited, unsure if anything else would happen. Finally, my mom walked over to the tree.

"I think it worked," she said.

"Did we get it on camera?" Dad asked Shane.

"I don't know. What *was* that?"

"Did you see it?" Noah asked me.

I nodded. We let go of each other's hands and moved toward the tree together.

"Is it over?" asked Avery. "Was that the end?"

I could hear Charlotte Pickens's voice clearly in my head. *There is no end.*

twenty-two

Applying eyeliner while someone is pounding on the walls below you is no easy task. After my tenth attempt at leaning into the mirror and trying to draw a straight line, I gave up and went downstairs.

"You look great, honey!" Mom said from the sofa. She closed a magazine and smiled at me.

"I would look a lot better if I could have a minute of peace!" I said, staring in the direction of my dad.

He stopped his hammer in midswing. "Sorry about that. I'll be done in just a second." He eyed my dress. "It's a little tight, isn't it?"

I looked down at the white satin gown I had chosen for Homecoming. Avery had gone to the mall with me the week before, pulled it off the rack and declared that it was perfect. I agreed and did my best to help her find an equally perfect dress in return. She had politely tried on everything I suggested but ended up choosing a lavender silk gown I hadn't even noticed.

"I think it looks lovely," Mom said. "And the tiara is a nice touch."

"The theme is 'Masquerade Ball.' I have a mask to go with it."

Shane poked his head in. "What time will Noah be here?"

I tried not to groan. Shane was more interested in when Noah's mom would be arriving. Trisha and Shane had become nearly inseparable in the two weeks since Charleston, something that had seemed sweet at first but was quickly becoming annoying. Shane spent all his free time with Trisha, talking about Trisha or planning elaborate dates with Trisha. He'd also decided that I was his official female perspective, which meant I had to approve every shirt, pair of shoes and spray of cologne he wore before he would leave on a date. It was strangely exhausting.

"Noah will be here any minute, so I need to finish getting ready." I looked at Dad. "Done?"

"Last nail," he said, turning back to the wall.

My parents had decided to stay in South Carolina for a while. They called it their "five-year plan" and said it was time to establish a home base. They would still travel, but now we would have a place to come back to. Dad was celebrating by covering every square inch of wall with framed pictures from his memorabilia collection. He'd dragged the dusty storage bins out of the garage and spent the weekend meticulously planning where each picture would be placed.

"A little to the left, dear," Mom said from the sofa. Dad examined the black-framed copy of the channel guide, nodded and moved his nail over slightly.

It was nice seeing them together in the same room. After our experiences in Charleston, something seemed to shift between my parents. Mom wanted to actively research "intelligent hauntings," an idea Dad vehemently opposed.

"Don't you think it's time to expand our research?" Mom asked him.

"No," came his firm reply. "We will not open ourselves up to ridicule. This field is difficult enough without throwing crazy, new-age mysticism into the mix."

"I'm not talking about mysticism," Mom replied. "I'm simply talking about being open to new possibilities."

But Dad wouldn't hear it. In his mind, what had happened simply needed to be studied patiently and thoroughly in order to discover the reasonable explanation behind it all. Examining the footage proved impossible, though. When we sat down to go over Shane's video footage, the tapes were blank. Not one image existed of the Circle of Seven ceremony. Instead of dancing lights, our monitors displayed black static. I knew what I had seen, though, and didn't need videotape to confirm my experience. Neither did Mom.

But while Mom moved further away from the ideas she once held, Dad was digging in his heels. He seemed to forget that our house had been ransacked and that mysterious lights had encircled us. I hoped he would start sharing Mom's new way of thinking, but if he didn't, I hoped that at least my parents could accept each other's opinions.

I returned to my room to finish getting ready. I hadn't decorated my walls yet, but it definitely felt like my space with its piles of clothes dotting the carpet and all of my things finally unpacked. It had been nice sleeping in my own bed over the past two weeks. I had been sleeping soundly, without dreams. After everything happened, I kind of hoped I would have just one more, something short and happy to let me know that everything was good with Charlotte Pickens and her parents.

I mentioned it to Noah, and he told me that it was a better sign not to have any more dreams.

"It means they've all moved on," he said. "And wasn't that the point?"

I agreed that it was. Then I agreed to go to Homecoming with him. It wasn't a date, exactly. Avery was actually the one who asked him out. She had stopped by AV class at the end of the day and mentioned the dance to Noah, who said he wasn't planning on going. "But you have to go!" Avery said. "I've worked so hard on this dance. You can come with me and Charlotte."

So that's how it was decided. The three of us would drive over together as friends, but I was secretly hoping that Noah and I would get some time alone together. I liked him, and my feelings had only grown since Charleston. He had seen my family at work and hadn't run in the other direction, and that counted for something. But two weeks had passed, and the only time we'd had to really talk was during AV class, where our conversations were constantly interrupted by the work we had to do. I couldn't tell yet if Noah saw me as anything other than a friend. Homecoming might change that, I thought.

"Avery's here!" Mom called up the stairs.

"Oh, good," I said when Avery walked into my room. "I need help pinning this thing in my hair." I handed her the little tiara and a handful of bobby pins and sat on my bed.

She began to pull my hair back. "You sure about this? People might think you're making a statement about who should be Homecoming queen."

"It's part of my overall costume," I said. "Trust me."

"I always do," she murmured.

"You look great, by the way."

"Thanks. This color suits me, I think."

I smiled. "It really does."

Charlotte Pickens's last whispered words to me didn't make sense at first. It took me a while to realize that she was actually giving me a message for Avery, one that I passed along a week later, after everything had calmed down a little.

We were at my house, watching the thermal camera footage from Giuseppe's. "She said that forgiveness has its own color," I told Avery. "She said that it appears as a unique shade of purple."

"When did she say this?" Avery asked.

I still wasn't prepared to tell people what had happened to me. It wasn't that I thought they would doubt me. It was just something that felt private, something meant for me alone. Instead of revealing my experience at the tree, I told Avery that I'd had another dream in Charleston. It wasn't exactly a lie, I reasoned. In many ways, it had been dreamlike and surreal.

"Will Jared be at the dance tonight?" I asked. Avery was finishing up with my hair, so I couldn't see her face.

"Maybe. He said he might stop by toward the end."

"Everything still good with you two?"

"Yes. A little awkward, I guess, but good." Avery stood in front of me and examined her work. "This side is uneven," she said. She began pulling pins from my hair. "I guess the weird part is how other people react to seeing me talking to him," she continued. "I feel as if I have to justify being his friend or something."

I liked seeing Jared at school every day. He didn't eat lunch with us or anything, but Avery went out of her way to make sure people knew he was not to be treated badly. She even approached Harris Abbott, the captain of the football team, and asked him to pass the message along to the rest of the football players: Jared James was not responsible for Adam's death.

I had been watching my classmates closely, looking for a change in how they treated Jared. So far, things had improved only slightly, but it was better than nothing.

"Okay. Done." Avery smiled. "You look very regal, Charlotte."

I stood up and curtsied. "As do you."

She laughed. "I'm not going for regal. My mask has feathers."

The Homecoming theme had generated a lot of buzz, as well as competition. In addition to crowning the traditional king and queen, we would also be voting on the masks, determining who had the most creative, the most unusual and the overall best. I knew some of the art classes had been devoting time to the project, mainly because Bliss Reynolds did a segment on it for the news.

I had another run-in with Bliss about a week after the Charleston incident. I was alone at my desk in the AV room, watching some of the daily footage, when Bliss sat down next to me.

"Rumor has it you're the reason why Avery and Jared are friends again," she said.

"I hadn't heard those rumors," I replied. I was focused on my work and didn't feel like being bothered, but Bliss didn't get the hint.

"Yeah, well, this school is fueled by them." Bliss sighed. "Like the ones that started after Adam died."

Now she had my attention. I paused the video I was watching and turned to her. "What rumors?"

"The ones about Jared, about how he caused the car crash." She shook her head. "I didn't believe them, of course. I guess people needed someone to blame. But when I spoke out about it, when I said it wasn't true…" Her voice trailed off. "People only listen to the pretty girls."

"What are you talking about? You're pretty, Bliss. You know you are."

She gave a short, bitter laugh. "Let me rephrase that. People only listen to the popular girls, girls like your sweet little friends."

I was confused. What was Bliss trying to say? And why was she trying to say it to me?

"Bliss—"

She stood up. "Forget it, okay? Just forget it. I don't know why I even tried to talk with you."

"Bliss, whatever I did that made you hate me, I'm sorry. It was unintentional."

For a split second, I thought I saw her eyes soften. But just as quickly, it was gone.

"Do you know how hard I've worked to make friends here? To gain a little respect and be taken seriously? And then you swoop in, a new girl from nowhere, and you're all anyone wants to talk about. 'Charlotte's so cool, Charlotte's so nice.' It's all I hear!" Bliss looked close to tears. "Well, enjoy your moment in the sun. Be careful, though. Sooner or later, everyone gets burned."

She walked off, leaving me to wonder what, exactly, had happened to her to make her feel burned. She hadn't spoken to me since that day, and I hadn't tried to speak to her. Whatever was going on with Bliss, it was hers to deal with it.

Avery and I were doing a final examination of our makeup when the doorbell rang. I hurried to find my mask, which I'd finished that morning. I knew most of the girls were masquerading as black cats or sequined devils, and I wanted to be different. I had taken a simple white mask and painted it silver, then decorated the edges with rhinestones. I helped Avery fasten on hers, which was covered with small purple feathers, and she helped me on with mine. Then we went downstairs.

Noah looked amazing. He was dressed in a white tux, and I felt my stomach flutter as I caught a glimpse of his green eyes behind his white mask. As Avery and I descended the stairs, my mom and Trisha took pictures. Noah smiled and handed each of us a rosebud corsage. "Great masks," he said. He tried to help me pin mine on, but he kept fumbling, so I did it for him. Avery pinned on her own corsage. After posing for another hundred pictures, the three of us were ready to leave. Avery and I linked arms with Noah and headed out to the driveway. My parents had finally agreed to let me drive their BMW but had been clear that it was just for one night. Avery climbed in the back while Noah took the passenger seat.

"If I didn't mention it before, you look incredible," he said.

"Thanks," I replied. "So do you."

"The little crown thing is cool, too."

I thought about why I had chosen my costume. It was ironic, really, that I was using a mask to reveal who I really was.

"It's an important part of the outfit," I said as I put the car in Reverse.

"A princess?" Noah asked.

"I'm not just a regular princess," I told them. "I'm a paranormal princess."

"What's the difference?" Avery wanted to know.

I smiled as I drove away from the neighborhood with my

two best friends and turned toward Main Street. It felt as if I was headed toward something more than just a normal Homecoming dance. It felt as though I was moving toward a whole new beginning.

"The difference is that I'm not normal," I said. "And I really, really like it that way."

★ ★ ★ ★ ★

Mara Purnhagen

Kate is confused when she arrives at Cleary High
to find the building's been "tagged" with a life-size
graffiti mural, and her friend Eli has gone missing....

Available now wherever books are sold!

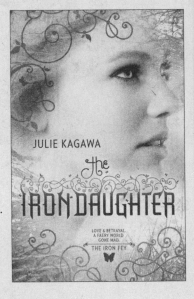
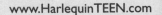